LOVE I

"It was all my fault," he whispered. "I'll never forgive myself – even if you can find it in your heart to forgive me."

"I can't," she said huskily. "I'll never, never forget tonight."

Distraught, he did not know what to say. He only knew that the sight of her with her hair falling about her shoulders, tears streaming down her face, affected him as nothing ever had in his life before.

"Dorina," he whispered, "Dorina – "

But her sobs did not cease, and comforting her became the most important thing in the world.

Forgetting everything except the bewildering sensation in his heart, he reached out to put his arms round her, pulling her against him.

The next moment his lips found hers.

The Barbara Cartland Pink Collection

Titles in this series

1. The Cross of Love
2. Love in the Highlands
3. Love Finds the Way
4. The Castle of Love
5. Love is Triumphant
6. Stars in the Sky
7. The Ship of Love
8. A Dangerous Disguise
9. Love Became Theirs
10. Love Drives In

LOVE DRIVES IN

BARBARA CARTLAND

Barbaracartland.com Ltd

First published on the internet in 2005 by
Barbaracartland.com

ISBN 1-905155-09-3

The characters and situations in this book are entirely imaginary and bear no relation to any real person or actual happening.

Printed and bound in Great Britain by CLE Print Ltd.
of St Ives, Cambridgeshire.

THE BARBARA CARTLAND PINK COLLECTION

Barbara Cartland was the most prolific bestselling author in the history of the world. She was frequently in the Guinness Book of Records for writing more books in a year than any other living author. In fact her most amazing literary feat was when her publishers asked for more Barbara Cartland romances, she doubled her output from 10 books a year to over 20 books a year, when she was 77.

She went on writing continuously at this rate for 20 years and wrote her last book at the age of 97, thus completing 400 books between the ages of 77 and 97.

Her publishers finally could not keep up with this phenomenal output, so at her death she left 160 unpublished manuscripts, something again that no other author has ever achieved.

Now the exciting news is that these 160 original unpublished Barbara Cartland books are ready for publication and they will be published by Barbaracartland.com exclusively on the internet, as the web is the best possible way to reach so many Barbara Cartland readers around the world.

The 160 books will be published monthly and will be numbered in sequence.

The series is called the Pink Collection as a tribute to Barbara Cartland whose favourite colour was pink and it became very much her trademark over the years.

The Barbara Cartland Pink Collection is published only on the internet. Log on to www.barbaracartland.com to find out how you can purchase the books monthly as they are published, and take out a subscription that will ensure that all subsequent editions are delivered to you by mail order to your home.

If you do not have access to a computer you can write for information about the Pink Collection to the following address :

Barbara Cartland.com Ltd.
240 High Road,
Harrow Weald,
Harrow HA3 7BB
United Kingdom.

Telephone & fax: +44 (0)20 8863 2520

THE LATE DAME BARBARA CARTLAND

Barbara Cartland who sadly died in May 2000 at the age of nearly 99 was the world's most famous romantic novelist who wrote 723 books in her lifetime with worldwide sales of over 1 billion copies and her books were translated into 36 different languages.

As well as romantic novels, she wrote historical biographies, 6 autobiographies, theatrical plays, books of advice on life, love, vitamins and cookery. She also found time to be a political speaker and television and radio personality.

She wrote her first book at the age of 21 and this was called *Jigsaw*. It became an immediate bestseller and sold 100,000 copies in hardback and was translated into 6 different languages. She wrote continuously throughout her life, writing bestsellers for an astonishing 76 years. Her books have always been immensely popular in the United States, where in 1976 her current books were at numbers 1 & 2 in the B. Dalton bestsellers list, a feat never achieved before or since by any author.

Barbara Cartland became a legend in her own lifetime and will be best remembered for her wonderful romantic novels, so loved by her millions of readers throughout the world.

Her books will always be treasured for their moral message, her pure and innocent heroines, her good looking and dashing heroes and above all her belief that the power of love is more important than anything else in everyone's life.

“*Love travels at the speed of light.*

Barbara Cartland

CHAPTER ONE
1895

Dorina Radford eyed the tennis net, then concentrated on the ball as she prepared to serve.

The mixed doubles match had been very finely balanced. The first set had gone to Dorina and her partner, Pierre Laforge. The second set had gone to their opponents.

Now Dorina was serving for the match.

She paused a long time, until she was sure she had the stroke exactly right.

It might only be a private match in the grounds of the Laforge mansion, just north of Paris. Her opponents and audience might only be guests of the house party arranged by Monsieur and Madame Laforge, and her partner might only be their son.

But none of this would deter her from giving the serve everything she had. It was Dorina's way to throw her whole self into whatever she did. Even the most inconsequential action was performed with total concentration and determination.

It was the only way to achieve success.

Her father had told her that, and he had every reason to know. Starting from nothing, he had created an industrial empire. Industry was booming in England, and he was one of the driving forces behind it.

Dorina swung her arm and watched with satisfaction as the ball flew over the net and straight between the other two.

An ace!

"Game, set and match to Monsieur Laforge and Mademoiselle Radford."

Cheers and applause from the spectators. Pierre and Dorina shook hands before advancing to the net to shake hands with their opponents.

One of the spectators regarded Dorina judiciously.

"An excellent tennis player," he observed. "An athlete, tall, slim, strong. In short, the new woman."

"Hmm!" said his companion. "To my mind, the new woman is too much like a man. Where is her femininity? Where is her grace? Where is the interest in fashion, without which no woman is truly a woman? Where is her – ?"

His hands described a figure eight.

"True," his friend conceded. "She has none of these qualities."

They exchanged shrugs.

"But her father is very rich," one of them conceded.

They nodded.

Dorina, passing close by, saw both the shrugs and the nods, and understood them.

She was used to being regarded as a bit of an oddity. In fact, she supposed that she *was* one.

Because her father had no son he had been determined that his daughter should follow him when he retired.

That made things far more difficult for her than they would have been to an ordinary girl.

John Radford had become one of the wealthiest and

most important men in the business and industrial world in the whole of England.

He had, unlike many of his contemporaries, concentrated not only on England, but also on the countries abroad, to which he hoped to export the goods he made.

Since he saw Dorina as the future of the firm, he had made her start learning foreign languages when she was ten.

As she grew up she learned more and more, sometimes residing in England, but often travelling abroad to perfect her languages.

She was very proud of the fact that she could speak and be understood in France, Spain, Italy, Germany and Holland.

She knew that her father was proud of her, but she would have liked to spend more time with him. Sometimes he would come abroad to visit her, but even then his mind seemed to be on the work he had left behind at home.

Last year, while they were together in Rome, he had said,

"I made up my mind, when I was very young that I would not only be very rich but, if possible, the richest man in the whole country."

"Papa!" she had exclaimed.

"It's no use looking shocked, my dear. In business the amount of money you make is the gauge of how successful you are. I wanted to be the richest man in England, and now I think that's what I have become."

"But you have nothing else in your life but your work," she had protested. "Mama has been dead for more than ten years now, and I think you should have married again. Then you might have had a son to train up for your empire."

"No," he said firmly. "That could never be. I gave my

heart to your mother and she gave her heart to me. No one can ever take her place in my life, even if it was an angel from Heaven."

For a moment his face was sad. But then he smiled at her.

"Besides, why should I need a son? I've got you."

Most men would not have regarded a daughter in such a light, and the knowledge that he valued her so highly warmed Dorina's heart.

But soon after that, he had left her to return to London. When she protested he said,

"No one can do what I do, as well as I do, although, in time, I'm sure you'll give me plenty of competition. Therefore you understand, my dearest, that I have to go home. I have to make the people I employ do it my way and not theirs."

Dorina had laughed and kissed him.

"You are doing too much, Papa," she had chided him. "When I finish here I'm going to learn the business so well that you can put your feet up and rest."

On her trips home he would take her around his factories and foundries, showing her the iron and steel works with which he created the goods that he supplied to the railways.

He made tracks, girders, carriages and engines. From the first moment Dorina was thrilled with everything, the size, the noise, the blaze of the furnaces. It might be 'unfeminine', but there was something about this bellowing, controlled ferocity that excited her.

She learned everything she could, and because she was truly interested she learned quickly. Her father was delighted with her progress, although he said,

"You think you're getting to know the business now,

but when you really concentrate you'll find out that there are a hundred more things to learn."

"I can't wait to start," she had told him firmly.

Now she was on her way home for the last time, ready to take her place beside her father, as they had both dreamed for so long.

She had returned through Germany, Italy and France on a trip that was, in a way, her farewell to a life of leisure.

She was entertained by the parents of girls who were more or less her own age, whose fathers had been negotiating with Mr. Radford.

"I think you must have been not only the cleverest man in Europe," Dorina wrote to him once, "but also the most charming, because I am overwhelmed with invitations wherever I go."

Her father wrote back saying he was very proud to have received letters from those who had entertained her, who said she was not only pretty and charming, but also as intelligent as they expected his daughter to be.

And brains mattered to Papa, she knew that. So it was lucky that she had some.

When she left here she would go first to the house her father owned in London, where he maintained his society and government connections that were sometimes useful to him. Then she would travel to their real home in Birmingham, where he had a house close to his main factories. There they would work together.

Dear Papa, she thought. They loved each other so much, but they had been parted too often. In future everything would be different.

Now, as she walked back from the tennis court, she found Sophie Laforge walking beside her, asking her about the gown she would wear at the ball this evening.

"It will be a marvellous ball," the French girl said. "Papa is celebrating his horses winning three races last month."

"Then I must be very smart," Dorina replied. "To make quite certain, I plan to wear a dress I bought in Paris."

"Then you will certainly be smart," Sophie said, and the two girls laughed together.

As they went into the house, a servant appeared to say there was a gentleman from England in one of the sitting rooms who had asked to see Mademoiselle Radford.

Dorina looked at her in surprise.

Without saying anything to her friend, she hurried into the house.

As soon as she opened the door to the sitting room, she recognised Mr. Johnson, her father's second in command.

The elderly man stood up as she approached and took one of her hands in both of his.

"I am afraid, Miss Dorina," he said, "that I bring you bad news."

Dorina stared at him.

"Papa is not well?" she questioned.

There was a moment's pause before the man said,

"It is with the deepest regret I have come to tell you that your father died two nights ago. He had a heart attack. There was nothing the doctors could do."

Dorina felt herself turn cold inside.

For a moment it was impossible for her to answer him.

She sat down on the sofa.

"I am sorry to have to bring you this bad news," Mr. Johnson said sitting down beside her. "As you can imagine we feel we have lost not only a great businessman but someone who was our friend who helped us in every possible way he could."

"How could Papa have died so unexpectedly?" Dorina sighed, "when I was on my way to see him?"

"The doctors said his heart gave up because he insisted on overworking himself, as he had all his life," Mr. Johnson replied. "If he had lived, he would have been an invalid, unable to work."

"He would have hated to do nothing," Dorina said almost as if she was speaking to herself.

"Of course he would. And now I have to tell you what he said to me only a short while ago."

"What is that?" Dorina asked.

"I think he must have had some premonition of trouble, because, in a strange way, he was prepared for it."

"How do you mean?"

"He sent for me, and a few of the others who held responsible positions, and told us that if anything happened to him, we must carry on with his business as he would have done himself. The person who would inherit his money and, he said very positively, his position, was to be his daughter."

Dorina stared at him but she did not speak.

"We all agreed that we would support you in every way, and do our best to carry on as he would have wished."

"But how can I take my father's place? He was going to train me, but he never had the chance. I know nothing."

"But you will have all of us to help you. He never had any doubts that you could do it. If only you could have heard him talk. He was so proud of you."

Suddenly Dorina burst into tears. She had kept emotion at bay until then, but when Mr. Johnson spoke of her father's pride in her she could bear it no longer. She buried her face in her hands and sobbed.

After staring at her for a shocked moment the old man put his arms about her and drew her head onto his shoulder.

"There, my dear!" he said. "It's how we all feel."

There was the sound of the door opening, and they both looked up quickly to see their hostess standing before them.

Mr. Johnson rose quickly.

"Excuse me, madame. I have come from England to tell Miss Radford that her father is unwell, and she should return without delay."

There was an immediate flurry of sympathy and arrangements. Madame Laforge insisted that Mr. Johnson must have something to eat while Dorina's maid did her packing. He accepted gratefully.

Dorina hurried upstairs, wondering why Mr. Johnson had pretended that her father was still alive. She had not missed the slight shake of the head that he had given her, warning her to stick to the story.

She was too much in turmoil to feel the depth of her own grief, but she knew that soon she would have to confront it. The father she had loved despite their separations, whom she had longed to join, was gone for ever. Now the dream of working together was shattered, and she would never see his pride as she carried on his work.

But she could not allow herself to mourn just yet. That would come later, when there was nobody to see her.

She slipped downstairs to join Mr. Johnson, who was eating enthusiastically.

"I have been travelling for two days," he said. "I slipped away at once and went straight to Calais to come and find you."

"Why did you not tell them that Papa is dead?" she asked.

"Because there are things we need to discuss, and decisions to make before too many people know the truth.

Your father died in Birmingham which is fortunate, because in London it would have been harder to keep his death a secret. Everyone, except the medical staff, believes that he is merely unconscious.

"By now his body will have been taken to the nearby Chapel of Rest, but the nurses will remain on duty as though he were in his own bed."

"But why the secrecy?"

"Your father was so important that the vultures will start circling when news of his death gets out."

"Yes, I see," Dorina murmured. "We must plan to defeat them, and not even be seen arriving in England together. You can tell people that I was too far away for you to reach me, but you have written to inform me of my father's death and I will doubtless return to England as soon as possible. But in the meantime you will carry on the business until I arrive."

"And then you will lead us," he said. "As your father did."

"Yes, but not at once. I want to learn about business first, so for the moment I will leave it to you to carry on exactly as if Papa was still alive."

"But what do you plan to do in the meantime?" he asked.

"I will tell you that on the journey home," she said. "We should be leaving very soon."

Monsieur Laforge provided his own carriage to take them to Paris, and everyone turned out to wave them off, with many expressions of good will.

They managed to secure sleeping cars on the night train from Paris to Calais. After eating dinner in the restaurant car, they retired for the night. Now that the first shock had passed, Dorina felt dragged down by grief and was unwilling to talk, or even to think any more tonight.

When her maid had made her comfortable and bade her goodnight, Dorina sat up in bed.

'I have simply got to make a success of this,' she told herself. 'Even though I'm quite certain the men who work for Papa will think I am too young, too pretty and too stupid to take his place.

'Yet I am sure he will help me from Heaven, and I will use the brains he always said I had. Then I will carry on his work and his achievements will not be lost.'

She got out of bed and went to the window, looking out at the darkened countryside that was swiftly passing by.

She looked up at the sky.

'Help me, Papa, help me,' she prayed. 'Wherever you are, tell me what I am to do. Oh, why couldn't you have waited just a little longer and been at home to welcome me? Already I miss you so much.'

*

Next morning she and Mr. Johnson ate a quick breakfast as the train covered the last miles to Calais.

"In many ways your father succeeded by being first in whatever he undertook," he told her. "We are making a train now that will be in advance of anything on the market. And, of course, there is his pet scheme."

Dorina gave a rueful smile.

"You mean the idea of a horseless carriage? Dear Papa, he was so set on that idea. Nothing would convince him that it simply isn't possible."

"He always said that it was the way of the future," said Mr. Johnson, "and that was his strength, that he could see what the future held for engineering."

"You don't mean that he's given his factories over to pursuing this crazy dream?" Dorina asked, startled.

"Oh no, we're still turning out the solid goods that

have been the firm's bedrock. The horseless carriage is simply a research project at Birmingham. It's been kept very secret because so many other people are looking into the same thing, and he wanted to be the first."

"But surely it isn't possible?"

"Once people said rail travel was impossible," Mr. Johnson reminded her. "Yet here we are, tearing about the world behind steam engines, going as fast as thirty miles an hour. You will scarcely believe this, but when the first passenger train ran, sixty years ago, there were those who predicted that the human frame could not endure a speed of thirty miles an hour. They said we would explode. But we didn't. Who knows what else is possible?"

"Who knows?" Dorina murmured. "Well, it will certainly surprise a lot of people to see me carrying on Papa's business, because I am a woman."

She laughed as she added,

"Most people, especially the English, think women are pretty little things with no brains."

"And you're going to prove them wrong?" he asked admiringly.

"I am going to have to find out first what I should have done ages ago – that is, how a businessman thinks, plans and makes decisions."

"Won't this turn out to be rather a hard life for you?" he pondered. "You're at the age when a young woman should be enjoying herself, buying beautiful dresses, having young men compete for her."

"I don't feel much like enjoying myself with Papa just dead. Still, I know what you mean. But that life isn't for me. Maybe I'll never marry. Papa has left me a sacred trust, and I won't let him down."

For a moment the softness left her face, replaced by a look of steely determination that startled Mr. Johnson.

On the journey across the English Channel he asked,

"What exactly do you plan to do when we reach England?"

"Discover all I can, so that I'm fit to take over."

"Wouldn't it be enough for me to teach you?"

"I shall want you to teach me, but I need to see everything from a different angle first. Who were Papa's greatest rivals? I need to know all about them if I'm going to beat them at their own game."

"The one who matters most is the Earl of Kennington."

"I've heard Papa mention him. It always surprised me that an Earl should be in trade."

"His father was awarded the title as a reward for his services to the country."

"I see. A title for him, but not for Papa?"

"I think he could have had a title if he had wanted one. There were hints that a large donation to a political party might work wonders. He wasn't interested. He said titles were a waste of time, and he had better uses for his money."

She laughed.

"I can just hear him saying it."

"We're nearly there," he said, looking at the white cliffs of Dover that were growing nearer.

"Remember to take no notice of me," she reminded him. "The press know your face and if they see me with you it will start speculation about my father. From here on, we travel apart, you to Birmingham, me to London and Papa's house."

"Your house now," he reminded her. "Remember the servants know nothing about his death. I'll keep things going in Birmingham and wait to hear from you."

"If I am in any trouble I'll contact you," Dorina

promised. "Otherwise I'll lie low for a while."

"Trouble?" A frown creased his forehead and there was an uneasy note in his voice as he asked,

"Miss Radford, exactly what are you planning to do?"

An impish smile touched Dorina's lips.

"It's probably best if I don't tell you," she said.

Mr. Johnson felt the hair begin to stand up on the back of his neck. He had seen that look before on the face of his late employer when he had just had a ground breaking idea that would either bankrupt the firm or make everyone's fortune.

*

Dorina woke very early, and for a moment she could not think where she was.

How did she come to be in her own bedroom in London when she should have been in France?

Then it all came rushing back to her – her father's death, the journey home, the decision she had taken.

Now was the time for action.

Her maid came in with the tea.

"Thank you, Bertha. Please lay out my plainest clothing."

Bertha stared. She was used to her mistress looking glamorous and elegant. The skirt and jacket that Dorina put on was dull and not very becoming.

Then she sat down at the dressing-table and brushed back her hair until it was away from her forehead and her cheeks. She pinned it securely at the back of her head.

"Whatever are you going to do, miss?" Bertha breathed.

"I'm going to get a job," Dorina said firmly.

As the butler served her breakfast Dorina said,

"Hastings, you know everything that's happening in London. Please tell me where the Earl of Kennington lives."

"You mean your father's competitor, miss?" he asked in tones of arctic disapproval.

"That's right. It's time I discovered a little more about him."

"He lives in Grosvenor Square, miss."

Plans were forming in her head. Bertha had just finished the unpacking, and gaped when Dorina instructed her to pack up again.

"Not very much, this time," she said. "And no fine clothes. The plainest things I have. I want to look businesslike.

'If I arrive with my luggage,' she thought to herself, 'I can say that I reached England early this morning and my friend in France had told me to go straight to the Earl of Kennington.'

"Will I be coming with you?" Bertha asked.

"Not this time. I want you to ask Hastings to fetch me a cab."

"Shall I tell him where it's going, miss?"

"No, I don't think so."

The Earl of Kennington's house was one of the largest in Grosvenor Square. She thought when she rang the bell that even the door looked rather grand and impressive.

It was opened by a footman, wearing a very smart uniform. Behind him stood the butler.

"I would like to see Lord Kennington," Dorina said, trying to sound firm and confident. "It is very important."

The butler frowned.

"Are you, by any chance, another secretary?"

"I beg your pardon?"

"Ever since his Lordship's secretary was taken ill, we've had a stream of applicants coming to this door." He added gloomily, "none of them any use."

Dorina suppressed the urge to smile broadly. So the Earl actually needed a secretary. This was better than she could have hoped.

"I think you will find that I am of some use," she asserted confidently.

"Then please come in."

He stared when he realised that she had two large bags with her, but indicated for the footman to help her.

"I arrived in England only this morning and came straight here," she explained hastily.

"Be so good as to wait in here while I speak to his Lordship. Your name, if you please."

"I am Miss Martin," she told him.

He opened the door of a small room near the hall, and when Dorina went in he closed the door behind her.

She had a look round the room thinking it looked richly furnished.

Clearly Lord Kennington was very rich, which meant that his business was profitable. But while her father had ploughed his profits back into the business, the Earl's father had expended some of his on a title.

She wondered which of them had been wiser.

She moved over to the fireplace and regarded herself in the mirror which hung above it.

She looked, she thought, very sensibly dressed, just right for a secretary.

But her hair had slipped forward a little and was very golden against her skin. She pushed it back and put on the glasses which she had brought with her.

They were actually her father's, but she thought they

gave her the impression of being older than she was. Also, she hoped, more intelligent.

The butler opened the door.

"His Lordship will see you now, Miss Martin."

This was it, the moment she had planned for.

She had a feeling that her prayer had reached her father, wherever he might be and he was somehow helping her.

Whatever happened, she must not let him down.

CHAPTER TWO

They walked down a passage on a very soft and expensive carpet.

She thought the pictures on either side of her were beautiful, while the furniture was outstanding.

The butler opened a door halfway down the corridor.

Then he said,

"Miss Martin to see you, my Lord."

Dorina realised, as she walked in, that it was his Lordship's study. A man was sitting at a very large writing-desk near the window.

The sun was glinting on a gold ink-pot.

As he put down the pen he was holding, it too glinted for a moment in the sunshine.

He rose and to Dorina's surprise, he was rather younger than she had expected him to be.

Somehow when she heard her father and other men talking about him, she had imagined he was at least forty-five and would have an aggressive manner.

But the man in front of her was, she thought, only thirty and surprisingly good-looking.

He had dark brown hair with a slight curl. His eyes were deep blue and had a brilliance that caught her attention. It was as though a light glowed from within him.

His figure was tall and broad shouldered and his legs very long. He seemed to radiate power, and cast everything else in the room into shadow.

He shook her by the hand saying,

"It is very kind of you to come and see me, and I need someone very badly at the moment."

He indicated a chair on one side of the fireplace and he sat down near it on a sofa.

"I'm in a rather difficult position as you have doubtless been told," the Earl began. "My secretary who has looked after me for several years and who, I may say, is completely indispensable, has been taken seriously ill.

"The doctor tells me it will be a long time before she can work again. I desperately need help, but so far none of the applicants has been suitable. I wonder if you're the person I'm looking for."

"I am certain of it," she replied with conviction. "I've just arrived in London from France. I have some knowledge of business, and I speak five languages fluently."

"Five languages!" the Earl exclaimed. Then he added in German, "Do tell me which they are."

Dorina realised that this was a test.

She replied immediately in German, and for a moment they conversed. She soon realised that his German was limited to the basics.

So was his French, she discovered, when they switched to that language.

She ended up by saying in Dutch,

"I hope that is what you wanted to hear."

The Earl stared at her in astonishment. Then he laughed.

"What was that?"

"Dutch."

"I don't believe you are true," he said. "How is it possible, looking as young as you do, that you should know so much?"

"It is a long story and rather boring," Dorina replied. "But I went to school in most of these countries and they encouraged me by asking me to visit their homes."

"All I can say is, as far as I'm concerned," the Earl said, "you are a miracle just when I needed one. I export a good deal of the goods I manufacture, and I must be able to deal with foreign buyers without stumbling over the language. What else do you speak?"

"Spanish and Italian," Dorina replied. "And you?"

"I have a smattering of those, but my skill is nowhere near yours," he added ruefully, "as I expect you have already realised."

"Yes I have" she replied promptly, but with a twinkle in her eye, and they both laughed.

"Then you will come and work for me?" he asked.

"I'll be glad to."

"About money – "

He named a sum that seemed trifling to Dorina. She could hardly have bought a hat for the amount that was to be the annual salary. But she knew that it was a generous wage for a secretary, and agreed without demur.

"Which of the many countries you have visited did you find the most enjoyable?" the Earl asked.

Now he was speaking in Italian.

Dorina answered him in the same language.

"I confess that I have more friends in France than in any other country," she said. "Therefore I find it more amusing to be in Paris than anywhere else."

"I can say the same," the Earl agreed. "When we have time you must tell me what you enjoy most, not only in Paris, but other places on the continent.

"In fact, I want to know all about you. How have you spent your life and why do you want this job? How can heavy engineering possibly be of interest to a young lady?"

"I am like no young lady you have ever known," Dorina replied.

"That I can believe."

"But as for telling you any more about myself – can we leave that until later? The important thing for you to know is whether I can do your job."

"You're right. Other things must wait their turn, but their turn will come, I assure you. Now, I'm going to take you to your office because there's a pile of letters we have to answer and which haven't even been opened. Although there are many things I want to talk to you about, business comes first."

"Of course it does," Dorina agreed.

They went out of the room and walked along the passage.

At the end of it the Earl opened a door into what she thought was a very tidy but rather dull office.

The secretary's desk was large, and set by a window which looked on to the garden at the front of the house.

As the Earl had said, the desk was piled high with work.

"I hope you will be comfortable here," he said. "If there's anything you need you must ask the butler and it will be brought to you at once."

"I think what I really need now," Dorina said, "is time to open all these letters."

"I've got very behind, as you can see," he said. "To catch up, I shall need to call on you at all hours. In fact, we haven't discussed your hours, and I was wondering – do I understand that you have nowhere to stay?"

"I came straight here from the train," she said.

"Would you consider it improper to stay in this house? I promise you I have no disgraceful intentions. It's purely a matter of business convenience."

"Of course," Dorina said. "It would suit me to stay here, and be close to the job."

"Then I'll tell my housekeeper to prepare a room for you, and your things will be taken upstairs."

"Splendid. Now let us get down to work."

"You don't know what music that is to my ears, Miss Martin. Well, you see the letters. The social ones are easy. I can tell you at once whether I wish to attend some ball or party. The other letters, which to me are the most interesting ones, refer to my business."

'Those are the ones which will interest me too,' Dorina thought, but she did not say so aloud.

She merely seated herself at the desk. There she saw a number of notebooks which seemed strange until the Earl said,

"The notebooks represent each of the companies of which I am the chairman. You will find in them the names of the members of the company and the managers both in this country and abroad."

Dorina smiled.

"That is very sensible," she answered. "It will save me asking you a great many questions which you would undoubtedly find exceedingly tedious."

"I don't know that I should," the Earl said. "I find my business far more interesting and exciting than the parties that I am invited to. They're all the same."

"Oh yes, too much social life can be so boring," she said without stopping to think. "That's why I'll enjoy working for you."

There was a silence. Looking up she saw the Earl regarding her with a touch of surprise, and realised that the working girl that she was supposed to be would have known nothing about social life.

Quickly she sat down at the desk, and picked up a letter opener, becoming very obviously absorbed in her task.

"Is there anything you want to ask me?" he enquired.

"Not at this moment," she said, her head buried in a letter. "Later I'm sure I'll have a hundred questions."

Without looking up she could sense that he was once more surprised. Such a handsome man was probably used to women who tried to keep him talking.

Without saying any more the Earl walked towards the door and opened it. He looked back at Dorina for a moment. Then he went out closing the door behind him.

When she was alone Dorina felt as if she wanted to jump for joy, because she had been so lucky in getting immediately to the one place she wanted.

'Everything is almost too smooth,' she thought. 'I must be careful not to slip up through sheer excitement.'

She took off her hat and tidied her hair not realising that when she sat down at the window again, the sunshine turned her hair to gold.

She had also taken off her coat.

Now wearing the silk blouse which was cool, she started to open the letters, feeling that each one was a treasure which would help her and was far more important for her than for the man to whom it was addressed.

She deliberately chose those which were obviously business letters.

She found two or three were exceedingly interesting and informative.

As she went on she found letters which told her very clearly that the Earl was extremely interested in the new vehicle which had just been invented, the horseless carriage.

She was delighted as she read how enthusiastic the writers were about this new vehicle.

'Maybe Papa was right,' she thought with rising excitement. 'And the horseless carriage really can happen.'

Many of the other letters were invitations and very pressing ones for his Lordship to attend dinner parties and dances both in London and in the country.

There were very large bills for new improvements to his house in the country and one which he had obviously just bought in Scotland.

It was under an hour later when she decided to take the business letters to the Earl.

She found him at his desk in the study where he had been before.

He looked up as she entered the room.

She had been so interested in what she had been reading that she had forgotten she had taken off her hat.

She had patted her hair into the usual way it was arranged without even looking in a mirror.

Only as the Earl stared at her, as she joined him at the desk was she aware he was looking at her hair.

She remembered she had almost hidden it when they first met.

He was however far too polite to make personal observations, although his eyes were on her hair.

As she joined him at his desk, he said,

"What have you found – anything of importance?"

"I think these three letters seem very important," Dorina replied. "They refer to this new invention – the horseless carriage – which certainly sounds something new and unusual."

The Earl smiled.

"That's what I thought too," he retorted. "Surely if we can travel quicker on the roads, just as a train travels quicker on its rails, it is a step forward."

"It's a fascinating idea," Dorina said. "I hope your Lordship will find time to tell me about it."

"Are you really interested," the Earl asked, "or are you being polite?"

"I'm really interested," Dorina told him. "Of course we all want to travel quickly."

She laughed as she added,

"What could be more exciting than being able to reach the country in perhaps half the time it takes now even with the swiftest horses?"

"Of that I am quite certain," the Earl pointed out, "and it is where the money is."

At that moment the door opened and the housekeeper entered. She gave Dorina a rather strange look, but bobbed politely and said,

"Your room is ready, miss."

"Has everything been done as I said?" the Earl asked.

"Yes, my Lord," said the housekeeper, wooden-faced. "The room has bolts on the door."

"Good. You take the point, Miss Martin? Even if I were to forget to behave like a gentleman, you have only to shoot the bolts across your door to be perfectly safe."

"I never doubted your Lordship," Dorina said, smiling. "But thank you."

As they went up the stairs the housekeeper said,

"A maid has been assigned to you, miss, and she is doing your unpacking now. She will see to anything you want."

They found the maid hard at work. She bobbed a curtsey to Dorina and introduced herself as Celia.

It was a fine, well-furnished room, looking out onto the extensive gardens. There was a large, comfortable-looking bed, and furniture of gleaming rosewood. Dorina was enchanted by her room.

There were two doors leading off the main room. One led to a bathroom and the other to a small ante-room where Celia would sleep.

Dorina reflected that the Earl had gone to a good deal of trouble to protect her reputation. It was just as well. Censorious tongues were always ready to wag where a young woman and a very handsome man were concerned.

And he *was* exceedingly handsome, she had to admit. It would be easy to become distracted from her main purpose.

But she would be strong, she resolved. She was here to work, not to indulge in daydreams about a young man's profile.

The maid brought her some lunch to her room, and then Dorina wrote a hasty letter to Mr. Johnson.

I have been taken on as secretary to Lord Kennington, Dorina wrote

Already I have learned that the horseless carriage may have more of a future than I thought. Please write to me at No.12, Grosvenor Square, addressing the letter to 'Miss Martin', and letting me know how advanced our research project is.

She sealed the letter and put it in her pocket. When she went downstairs the Earl was not there, so she slipped out of the house and posted her letter.

She returned to the house and was back in her office

before he appeared and they immediately got down to work.

By the end of the day she was more than ever convinced that she had done the right thing in coming here. The Earl's correspondence was as wide-ranging as his interests, and she could tell that she had impressed him with her intelligence and quick understanding.

"That will be all for today," he said at last. "I have worked you very hard, and I'm sure you would like a meal and a rest. I will see you in the morning."

He retired to his room with his valet, and an hour later he left the house wearing white tie and tails.

Dorina dined in solitary state, trying to keep her mind on what she had learned that day, but it was hard when her thoughts kept dwelling on the Earl.

Where had he gone, dressed for an evening's pleasure. And who had he gone to meet?

She forced herself to concentrate on the matter in hand and took some reading matter up to her room. That was when she made a fascinating discovery.

"Electricity!" she said awed. "The lights work by electricity."

"Oh yes, miss," Celia said. "His Lordship must have all the latest inventions in his home. You should see the things we've got in the kitchen."

"Electric? And they all work?"

"We – 'ell – " Celia became cautious. "His Lordship invented a washing machine, with an electric motor to turn the drum. The trouble is, the water keeps dripping on the motor, and then it gives a little explosion and dies."

"That must be very frightening," Dorina observed.

"Oh no, miss," Celia said cheerfully. "You get used to things exploding. Even the cat."

"The cat?" Dorina asked, beginning to laugh.

"Yes, Tiggy used to dive for cover, especially after the first time when his whiskers got singed. But now he just sits there and watches. And his Lordship always says sorry ever so nicely."

"Even to Tiggy?" Dorina asked, chuckling.

But Celia replied seriously, "especially to Tiggy. He says humans can understand, but a poor dumb animal doesn't know what's happening, and it's very kind of him to go on living here in the circumstances. Tiggy always gets extra special fish after an explosion."

As Celia helped her undress, Dorina considered what she had learned about the Earl. A picture was beginning to emerge of a loveable madman, for whose sake his servants would take explosions in their stride.

Even his cat was philosophical.

Her father too had always been wild for the latest inventions, but he had been profoundly serious about them. And while he had illuminated his factories by electricity, he had not bothered with his homes.

Nor could she imagine him apologising to his cat for singed whiskers.

At last Celia said goodnight and went to lie down in the ante-room.

Dorina went quietly to the door to make certain it was bolted. And now she saw something she had not noticed before.

The bolts were brand new.

It was clear that they had been attached to the door only that day.

Once again she was struck by the trouble the Earl had taken to observe the proprieties. By now the whole household must know that he could never burst into this room, even if he wanted to.

But Dorina remembered that she had gone out of her way to look plain to him. Perhaps this was his way of telling her that he could never want to burst in. She was perfectly safe because she did not attract him.

Then she recalled the expression on his face as he had glanced at her hair and suddenly she felt herself blushing from head to toe.

'Stop that!' she told herself sternly. 'You are here to learn about business and engineering and the horseless carriage and – and that sort of thing.'

She crept into bed and tried to read, but suddenly she could not concentrate. At last she put out the light and lay awake for a long time, her head whirling with thoughts.

But none of them was about horseless carriages.

*

Next day they both worked tirelessly. Dorina found it fascinating, but the hardest thing was not to let the Earl suspect how much she already knew.

When they had finished he went upstairs, and, as before, came downstairs dressed for an evening out.

But then there came a knock at the front door, and a letter was delivered to the Earl by hand.

"What a pity," he said. "My hosts have had to cancel the dinner at the last moment, owing to a family crisis. Here I am, dressed up with nowhere to go."

There was a silence as he looked at her and Dorina was suddenly very conscious of how dowdy she looked in the plain brown dress she had chosen to wear for work.

"Why don't you dine with me tonight?" he said. "Then we can continue our discussion, and between us we will invent marvellous things."

"I'm sure you can invent marvellous things without me," she said, laughing because her heart was soaring with pleasure.

"Thank you. I needed that encouragement."

"Why, particularly?" Dorina enquired.

"Because as hard as I try to keep in the lead, there are always men ready to race ahead of me."

"Nonsense!" Dorina exclaimed merrily. "Your Lordship is so clever that it would be impossible for people to catch you up, let alone beat you to the post."

The Earl laughed.

"Now you are cheering me up and I insist that you dine with me tonight. I'll wait for you here while you change. We could go to the Ritz if you like."

Plainly he meant to give her a treat, but Dorina said hurriedly,

"I'd rather go somewhere quiet, so that we can talk uninterrupted. I'd be rather shy in the Ritz in case your society friends came in."

Dorina was thinking that they might meet someone who would know her and give away her true identity.

"Very well," he said. "I will take you to dinner to a place I discovered a long time ago. It's by the river, very quiet and we could talk in peace."

"I would love to go," she said.

She was determined to dress very demurely, but she had forgotten that her gowns came from Paris.

Although she chose what appeared to be a very simple gown, but when she put it on, it still had that chic brilliance which the Parisian clothes always seemed to have.

It was black with touches of gold, and it seemed to make her hair appear even more golden too.

Also it made her skin look even paler and more beautiful than any other gown she might have worn. Because she thought it a mistake to wear any jewellery as she was merely a secretary, she only had two very small rings in her ears.

But as they were diamonds set in gold, they made her look even more beautiful than she would have done without them.

When she came down the stairs into the hall where the Earl was waiting for her, she would have been very foolish if she had not realised there was a glint in his eyes.

There was also a look of surprise as he realised that she was like no other secretary. He became thoughtful.

His carriage was outside.

When they got into it and the footman shut the door, the Earl said,

"I think it's time you told me the truth."

"The – truth?"

"Why are you trying to pass yourself off as an ordinary secretary, when you know very well that you are no such thing?"

CHAPTER THREE

Caught off-guard by the question, Dorina looked at him cautiously.

"I'm sure I do not know why you should ask that," she said, assuming an offended tone, hoping that it would put him off. "Have you any complaints about my work?"

"None at all, as you well know."

"I'm a good secretary?"

"You're an excellent secretary."

"Then that's all there is to be said."

"Oh no, it isn't" the Earl persisted. "My point is that you're *too* good. You're intelligent, you know the languages and you're obviously highly educated. Far from being an ordinary working girl, you're a lady."

"An impoverished lady," she supplied quickly. "I have to earn my bread and I don't fancy being a governess or a school-mistress."

"I thought impoverished ladies aimed for rich husbands," he observed.

"Rich husbands require dowries," she pointed out.

"Your brains and your beauty could be your dowry."

"A nice compliment, but a man with a ramshackle castle cannot repair it with brains and beauty," she said, remembering one particular suitor.

"Have you known many?" the Earl enquired with interest.

"One hears things, travelling around," Dorina replied vaguely.

She had made a bad slip, she realised, allowing him to know too much.

"I'm sure one hears about men on the look-out for money," he replied. "But not every man is a fortune hunter. Some can afford to marry for the woman's own intrinsic worth, and in that sense, you have much to offer.

"I'm surprised that you don't seem to have thought of it. What is it about working for me that sent you flying to my house?"

He was creeping too near the truth. Backed into a corner, Dorina responded with the first thing she could think of.

"How dare you!" she said in tones of fury.

The smile vanished from his face.

"What – ?"

"Do you have the unspeakable effrontery to suggest that I'm setting my cap at you? You think that's why I came to work for you? For shame, my Lord!"

"No – please, I didn't mean – "

"Or perhaps you think I'm hoping to be introduced to your society friends? Yes, that would be it. I could never aspire to an Earl, but he might have a banker or two among his acquaintances."

"I didn't – "

"Of course I shouldn't feel surprised that you feel free to pour scorn on me, alone and friendless as I am. What else can a poor girl expect?"

"I never poured scorn on you," he said desperately. "And I didn't say – "

"You implied!"

"I did not! How was I to know you were so dashed touchy?"

"A defenceless woman has to be touchy, as you put it," Dorina informed him in arctic accents. "Her reputation is at stake."

"Oh Lord!" he groaned, horrified at himself, at her and at the whole mess in which he suddenly found himself.

"Of course I risked my reputation when I agreed to stay in your house. If I had only known how that would be interpreted – *oooooh!*"

She rounded off the performance by bursting into violent sobs and burying her face in her hands. From his corner the Earl regarded her aghast, and then askance. Gradually a gleam of humour came into his eyes.

Unnerved by the silence, Dorina parted her fingers and looked through them to find him grinning at her.

"You can stop now," he said. "You've made your point."

"Have I?" She dropped her hands.

"Yes, you were very effective at first, but then you overdid it. Tears!"

"I don't see why you shouldn't believe my tears," she said indignantly.

"I'd believe them from anyone else, but not from the woman who discussed piston engines with me all afternoon. I'm sorry Miss Martin, perhaps I have been a little insensitive, but you must know that I never meant to imply any of the things you said."

"Yes, it was unkind of me," she said, relenting, "especially as you had someone put bolts on my door."

"I didn't 'have someone' put them on. I put them on myself. I hit my thumb with the hammer, too."

His aggrieved tone made her laugh and he joined in.

"I was only talking about how beautiful you are," he added. "But I suppose you'll take offence at that now."

"I promise not to. But there's nothing remarkable about my appearance."

"Nonsense. Looking as you do now, you would light up a Mayfair ballroom."

"Oh the dress!" she said lightly. "I told you I'd just come from France. I have very generous friends in Paris and this was one of their presents to me. You know that French clothes make all the difference."

She smiled as she added,

"Perhaps it's something you should pay attention to in your effort to develop new things and new ideas. After all, you've done shipping and trains, surely making an English woman outstanding should be somewhere on your list."

The Earl laughed.

"Trains are easy," he said. "The adornment of a woman might be a little beyond me. All I know is that you would be admired, even at Buckingham Palace."

"Although you may not believe it, I would rather be where we are going now than being entertained at Buckingham Palace."

He looked wary.

"Meaning you want to talk about piston engines again?"

"No," she said in a considering voice. "Tonight, I thought we might move on to variable steam pressure."

He laughed out loud, and there was a new note in his voice. She saw pure admiration in his eyes, and the air in the carriage seemed to sing. For a moment Dorina almost succumbed to it. She was going out to dinner with a handsome man who admired her. Why should she not enjoy herself?

But she was here to work, she reminded herself sternly. Any distractions were a betrayal of her father.

So she forced herself to change the subject, and spoke decisively,

"What I find so interesting is that you are always looking out for something different. That's very unusual in an Englishman. He is usually far too complacent and does not like change of any sort."

There was a slight pause before the Earl replied. He seemed to be a little disconcerted.

"That is unkind," he said at last, "but, I feel, true. We've tended to accept things as they've always been, and believed that because we are English we are right in everything we say and do."

Dorina laughed.

"Yes, I'm afraid that's how we are."

"It's something we have to change," he added firmly, "and, Miss Martin, that is what I intend to do."

"I think you've been very successful already," Dorina replied. "But you must realise that there is a great deal more for you to tackle."

"Are you challenging me?" the Earl enquired.

"Of course," Dorina said. "There's always room for improvement."

The Earl was silent for a moment.

Then he said,

"You are the most extraordinary young woman I have ever met. I'm sure you have thought seriously about what you are saying and I know it should be an inspiration to me, but why are you so anxious for me to do more?"

"That's easy. Because you *can* do it. Although I've only been with you a short while, I'm sure that you are capable of doing great things."

She felt, as she was saying this, as if the words were being put into her mouth.

Then she suddenly asked herself what she was doing.

She was here for the sake of her father's business and her father's memory. Yet she found herself trying to inspire the Earl to greater heights.

"But why are you so sure of that?" he asked, trying to see her in the gloom of the carriage.

"I don't know," she said slowly. "But I am – very sure."

The next moment she felt the carriage begin to slow.

"We're here," he said.

He sounded dazed, and almost relieved. Dorina too felt relieved. Something was happening that was carrying her away too fast.

She needed to stop and think, but how could she think when her heart was pounding?

The carriage had stopped. The door was being pulled open.

The Earl got out first and turned back to assist Dorina. She felt the warmth of his hands holding her, the sense of leashed power. Then he released her.

The restaurant was small, almost hidden away, but discreetly luxurious. The building was decorated with models of ships and fish, and the door through which they entered was graced with a sea serpent overhead.

They were shown to a table in an alcove that looked out directly on to the River Thames.

'This is certainly unusual,' she thought to herself, 'and that is exactly what the Earl is. Unusual. In fact, I've never known anyone like him. Not even Papa.'

He ordered their dinner and they settled down to talk. At first they discussed steam pressure and other engineering details, but gradually Dorina worked him round to talking about himself.

"Everyone thought," he said, "that because my father had a title and I inherited it, that I should merely be a social figure with no particular interest other than ballrooms and race meetings."

Dorina laughed.

"Then they certainly made a mistake," she said.

"And I intend to do more," he replied. "I like inventing things. It pleases me to think a train is going faster because I have thought of new improvements, which those who invented it did not think of.

"It's what I've wanted to do ever since I could remember. So far I have succeeded a little, but not as much as I want. There's still much to do with great new inventions still to come."

"You mean, like the horseless carriage?" Dorina asked. "So many of your letters are from people wanting to know about it, that it must be on the horizon."

"So people say," he agreed. "But just because everyone's talking about it doesn't mean it's about to happen. Of course I'm researching it, but so are a lot of others."

"So what will you say to those people who are asking you about it?" she wanted to know. "It's time we answered those letters."

"You're right. I'll write back, putting them off."

"But they're waiting for something from you. I can't believe that you've actually made no progress with this project."

"It won't hurt them to wait a little longer. What would really be damaging would be to announce a new product before it's ready. How my competitors would laugh at that!"

She had to admit that he was right. At the same time she felt rather disappointed that he would not tell her more.

"Now, that's enough about business," he said. "I want to talk about you."

For a moment she was wildly tempted. She was so happy here talking with him. It felt so right, so natural. They could talk some more, and grow closer –

Then warning bells sounded in her head. This was a luxury she must not allow herself. Not yet.

"I think that must wait until another day," she replied.

The Earl was silent for a moment. He seemed to be looking into the distance, as though coming out of a dream.

"The time seems to have rushed past," he said, "but of course we must talk again. I can honestly say I have enjoyed this evening enormously, far more than if I were dancing rather aimlessly round a polished floor with a young woman in my arms who only giggled when I spoke to her."

"Now you are being unkind," Dorina said. "I'm certain that unless you frightened her, she would have had a great deal to say. After all, you are who you are."

"Which is sometimes a disadvantage," the Earl retorted. "One is never quite certain if people are being complimentary to you as a person, or polishing up your title simply because it is something they would like themselves."

"I think if you have earned it," Dorina said, "it is something of which one should be very proud."

"Are you saying that to please me or because you really think so?" the Earl asked unexpectedly.

Dorina laughed.

"I really do think so, and it's a great thing that, in this

country at least, a man is honoured as he deserves. That's how your father earned his title."

"And I have only inherited it," the Earl replied.

"Yes," Dorina agreed, "but you've worked hard to keep your father's legacy alive."

It was late when they finally left the restaurant.

They were almost the last to leave. They had been talking so earnestly that the time seemed to slip by unnoticed.

"I find you fascinating," the Earl said, "and I want to go on talking and arguing with you until the morning sun breaks through."

"Then we would be very tired all day," Dorina said. "Come along we must go home."

The Earl paid the bill and they drove back to the house. Not a word was spoken on the journey home, but Dorina could sense him smiling at her in the darkness of the carriage.

When they were in the hall, Dorina said,

"Thank you, thank you for a most delightful evening. I enjoyed every moment of it."

There was a soft sound and a small creature brushed past her.

"It's Tiggy," the Earl said, picking up the cat. "Hallo, old fellow."

"How are your whiskers these days?" Dorina asked, scratching the tabby head.

"Ah, they've told you about that?" the Earl said with a grin. "Yes, he's an old soldier. He knows how to cope with my funny ways."

Dorina watched as the cat pressed closer to his master in a way that said more than words. This man had the gift of winning love, she thought.

Goodnight, my Lord," she said hurriedly. "And thank you again."

She went upstairs without looking back at him.

*

Next morning she hastened down to breakfast and then to her office.

There was no sign of the Earl, but she refused to admit to herself that she was disappointed.

She had lain awake thinking of him before falling asleep and dreaming of him. But that did not mean that she was in love, she assured herself. It was a natural reaction to a pleasant evening out with a charming man.

As usual there were a great number of letters which had arrived by the morning post.

Her mind was still elsewhere as she opened the first letter, and she scarcely noticed that the writing paper was rich and engraved not only with the address, but with a very important crest.

The letter read,

Darling Gerald,

I miss you terribly and long to be with you. You always say such wonderful things to me, and I lie awake at night thinking how happy we were that magical evening.

It is very boring being here in the country, with everyone talking about horses and racing, when I want to be with you.

I love you, I love you, and as soon as I am back in London I want you to tell me that you really love me.

Bless you and a thousand kisses,

Elsie.

With a sense of shock she realised that she had intruded on something private. Hurriedly she put the letter back into the envelope.

She wondered who Elsie was. It seemed strange for a young girl to write in such a way.

Perhaps it was an older woman.

Yes, she wrote like a woman of experience and the Earl evidently had a relationship with her that enabled her to write to him in such passionate terms.

Was this the reason why he seemed indifferent to virtuous young ladies of society? Because he enjoyed liaisons with women whose virtue was less outstanding?

The thought saddened her. But, after all, what did she know about him?

She put the letter discreetly with the others, and left it for him.

'If only he would return,' she thought. 'I would so like to talk to him.'

But when the butler, whom she had discovered was called Henly, brought in her morning coffee he told her that his Lordship would be out all day.

In fact, he did return in the afternoon, but only to go straight upstairs to dress for an evening out. Just before he departed again, he looked in on her with a smile.

"Are you managing all right?" he asked. "Good – I knew you could cope."

Then he was gone, without giving her a chance to reply.

She ate a lonely supper and retired early, feeling unhappy.

Next morning there was no sign of him when she started work and Henly confided that he had returned very late last night.

It was after lunch when she heard him come downstairs and go into his sitting room. Dorina went straight to him with the letters. Strictly speaking she knew she should have waited to be sent for, but something in her longed to see him.

As she entered he turned from where he was standing at the window.

"I have your letters for you," she said as she put them down on his desk.

She had arranged them with the private ones on the bottom.

Two of the letters were from English hostesses who wanted him to dine with them.

The third was the letter she had read the previous day.

To her surprise the Earl took this last letter, read it, then tore it into pieces and threw them into the waste-paper basket.

Dorina longed to ask him why he had not wished to answer the woman who had written with such desperate passion.

But she thought it best not to pry, which undoubtedly she had done by reading his very personal letter.

He was very businesslike that afternoon, and finished work early. He was giving a dinner party that evening.

Dorina wondered if Elsie would be there, sitting beside him, laughing with him.

Perhaps not, since he had torn up her letter.

But there would be many other women.

"Enjoy your party," she said as she left him. "But don't forget you're leaving early tomorrow morning to go to the races."

"I suppose I'll have to go," the Earl sighed. "I have a horse running in the third race. But there's really so much for me to see to here that I ought to stay. Yes I must go. I have friends expecting me."

She retired early and tried to sleep, but she could not

help being intensely aware of the noise of merriment coming up from the Earl's dinner party below.

She pictured him there, surrounded by beautiful women. Then she dived under the bedclothes and pulled the pillow over her head.

By the time Dorina reached her office the following morning, the Earl had left the house.

She wished she could have gone with him to the races.

'He is so different from the other men I have met,' she told herself.

But she did not want to explain the difference even to herself.

It was late in the afternoon and she was beginning to think she had finished all the work she had to do, when to her surprise, one of the footmen announced,

"A gentleman to see you, Miss Martin."

She looked up and saw it was Mr. Johnson.

She gave a cry of surprise and exclaimed,

"I was not expecting you. How wonderful to see you. Do tell me what you are doing here."

"I have come," Mr. Johnson began, "with extremely good news. In fact you will be astonished at what I have to tell you."

Dorina looked surprised and quickly sat down beside him.

"Tell me," she said eagerly.

"We've done it!" Mr. Johnson said.

"Done what?" Dorina asked.

"The horseless carriage," was his astounding reply. "We've created one and it works."

Dorina drew in her breath.

Then as Mr. Johnson finished speaking, she clasped

her hands together and bent towards him.

"I cannot believe what I am hearing!" she exclaimed.

"It's been a very hard job, to make a four-wheeled vehicle which will run on the roads and be propelled by gasoline. But we've done it.

"I received your letter on the very same day that we knew we had a success. It was like an omen. I knew I had to come and see you at once.

"Now that you know, I beg you to be careful. You have a rival here in this house. He must not guess how far advanced we are, in case it inspires him to complete his own work."

"I don't think there's much danger of that," Dorina said. "His project isn't very far advanced."

To her surprise, his face changed.

"On the contrary, he – "

"He what?" Dorina asked, beginning to feel uneasy.

"I suppose he has kept it from you, as he's kept it from most of the country. But the Earl's project is almost at the point of success."

Dorina stared.

"Surely not?"

"I learnt about it because a man who had worked for the Earl came to work for us because he was dismissed, he thought unfairly, and therefore came and told us everything."

Dorina drew in her breath.

"Tell me more," she said. "I want to know every detail."

"The Earl has been very clever. He has his private factory in a part of London which you would never visit. Certainly none of his smart friends would go there. He's nearly at the point of success, but he's managed to keep it a secret from everyone."

"Yes," Dorina said quietly. "He has."

He had refused even to confide in her, she realised.

She had thought they were drawing close, but all the time she had been nothing but an employee, to be told exactly what suited him and no more.

It hurt more than she would have believed possible.

CHAPTER FOUR

For a moment Dorina wondered sadly how he could have deceived her.

But then she remembered that she was here under false pretences. How could she blame him for keeping his secrets when she herself was keeping so many?

"What I came to tell you," Mr. Johnson said, "is that we're planning a big meeting in Birmingham, to which we will invite buyers from all over the world. There we will put our horseless carriage on display and gather orders ahead of our competitors. I'll write to you soon when I know more. But be prepared to come to Birmingham quickly."

"I will," she said.

"I know your father, if he were alive, would be thrilled and delighted that we have been so successful. I think it only right, if you agree, that if our great new invention is praised, as it will be, you take the credit of owning it and make everyone aware that your father unfortunately is no longer with us."

Dorina drew in her breath.

For a moment she almost felt as if the room was swinging round her.

She found it difficult to believe what she had heard and to realise the importance of it.

Then she told herself that she must not behave like a

frightened woman.

As her father's daughter, she must bravely face the future carrying on his great legacy.

And yet it flashed through her mind that she would be far happier if she remained as she was, with the Earl, growing closer to him.

Then she told herself she would not be a coward.

At last she managed to say,

"Of course I will do exactly what you want me to do. I can only thank you, as my father would have done, from the bottom of my heart. Have people not been curious as to where he is?"

"I told them he was abroad looking for new ideas and new inventions," Mr. Johnson said, "and, of course, everyone in their minds added – 'and new customers.'"

Then almost as if he thought the Earl might be listening, Mr. Johnson added,

"Are you quite certain Lord Kennington does not know who you really are?"

"Of course not," Dorina replied. "I came here as his secretary, and he has no idea I have any interest other than the work I am doing for him."

"Good. Let's hope it stays that way. I gather that his own vehicle is so far advanced that it might cause us problems if news gets out. As things are, we will soon have the world at our feet."

"Or perhaps *he* will," she murmured.

'I suppose,' she told herself, 'I ought to hate him, because if his car is at all good, it will take some of the glory away from me and Papa.'

However she did not say this aloud.

"Please arrange an increase in wages for all the men who are working on the horseless carriage," she said. "Our future depends on them, and I want them to feel appreciated."

"It will certainly do that," Mr. Johnson agreed. "May I say you are your father's daughter in thinking of other people as well as yourself?"

"Thank you," Dorina said.

"Perhaps I should go now. It would be better if the Earl does not find me here."

When he had left, Dorina sat silently thinking over what she had heard. She knew that this should be her proudest and happiest moment. But all she could think of was how the Earl had thrown dust in her eyes.

'He is cleverer than I thought him to be,' she thought.

In a strange way she found that she was almost as eager for his success as she was for her own, even though they were rivals.

She wished that she could discuss it with him, and no longer keep her true identity a secret.

'How close we might have grown, sharing the same ambitions,' she thought. 'Now, perhaps he will think I was spying on him.'

She could not bear that thought. She had found that there was something almost magical in being with him.

But now, how could things ever be right between them again?

After a while Dorina realised that she could not go on day dreaming all this time and went back to work.

But within a few minutes there was another interruption.

She heard the sound of voices in the hall. The butler seemed to be trying to restrain someone who would not be denied.

Then the door opened and a woman swept in.

She was very smartly dressed. The feathers in her hat fluttered as she shut the door behind her.

As she approached the desk she gave an exclamation and stared at Dorina.

"Where is Evelyn?" she asked, naming Dorina's predecessor.

"I am afraid Miss Barnes is very ill, so I have taken her place."

"Are you now his Lordship's secretary?" the woman asked in such a scathing voice that Dorina looked at her in surprise.

She thought she was deliberately being unpleasant.

"I have come," she said quietly, "to help his Lordship in an emergency. Fortunately that is what I am able to do."

"I should be very much surprised if you can," the woman answered. "I told him that I would be calling on him this morning. Where is he?"

"He has had to go out," Dorina told her.

"But I want to see him at once," the newcomer persisted. "In fact we had arranged to be together today, and that is why I came here as early as I could."

"I am sure his Lordship will be returning as soon as possible," Dorina replied. "In the meantime perhaps you would like to wait for him."

She spoke in a polite voice, but it was hard to keep her temper in the face of so much unpleasantness.

"He should have informed me," the woman went on accusingly, "that he required a secretary. I would have found him one who would be, I am quite sure, far more capable of doing his very difficult work than you are."

She was being very rude. But Dorina knew that in her position, it would be a mistake to be rude in return.

She therefore said,

"I am sure, madam, you know your way about the house and the butler will bring you any refreshment you require. I will tell his Lordship as soon as he arrives home that you are waiting for him."

"I will be very surprised," the woman retorted, "if you do anything efficiently. You are far too young and far too inexperienced for this work, and I will tell him so as soon as he comes back."

With that she went out slamming the door behind her.

Dorina was astonished that anyone so smartly dressed, who was obviously of some importance, should behave in such a way.

When a few moments later, the butler appeared she asked,

"Who was that lady? She was very upset not to find his Lordship at home."

Henly laughed.

"Upset, is the right word," he replied. "She's been scowling at me as if it is my fault he's forgotten the appointment."

"Who is she?" Dorina enquired.

"Lady Musgrove. She's been after his Lordship for some months. If you ask me she fancies herself as a Countess and there's not a person in this house who's not praying it won't happen."

"She certainly seemed annoyed and surprised to find me here," Dorina replied.

"Of course she was," Henly answered. "You're far too pretty for her Ladyship's liking, and I know now why she snapped at me in the drawing room."

Dorina laughed.

"Surely it cannot concern her who the Earl has as his secretary," she said. "He could hardly manage without one."

"Of course not," the butler agreed. "But Miss Barnes is about fifty. She's a good worker but she doesn't look as good as you do. You're like a bit of sunshine in the early morning."

Dorina laughed.

"That is the nicest compliment I have ever received," she said. "I would love to be a bit of sunshine, and I hope I've helped his Lordship with this huge amount of correspondence. Just look at what has arrived this morning and someone has to answer them for him."

"Well, her Ladyship thinks you're too pretty to be useful behind a desk," the butler said. "If you ask me it would be a disaster for us all if his Lordship married her, as she wants him to do."

Dorina could understand that.

After the way Lady Musgrove had spoken to her, she was quite certain that she could not manage the household in the way her mother had always done.

As she had said so often,

"If the servants are happy, their master is happy. Always remember that, darling, and it is something which should be written in every rich man's and woman's diary."

Dorina had laughed at the time and her father did too.

But she knew that all the servants at home were devoted to them both.

They had been unceasingly kind to her from the time she left the pram and toddled into the kitchen.

'Henly is right,' she thought to herself. 'The Earl must not marry a woman like that, who might not only offend his staff at home, but the people who work for him in other parts of the world. It was very important that the Earl should choose the right wife.'

But she did not allow herself to think too much about who the right wife might be.

She was still working on the correspondence, when Lady Musgrove reappeared.

"Exactly when did his Lordship depart?" she snapped.

"I am afraid I have no information," Dorina replied, "as he left before I came down to breakfast."

Lady Musgrove stared at her.

"Are you staying here in the house?" she asked in astonishment.

"When I applied for the job, I explained to his Lordship that I had only just returned home from the continent," Dorina told her. "He therefore offered me a room until I found somewhere else."

"All I can say is that you should do so as quickly as possible," Lady Musgrove replied. "It is not a good idea for people to think he has a young secretary who looks, to my mind, overdressed. That sort of thing is not good for his reputation."

Dorina drew in her breath.

For a moment she thought she should be as rude to Lady Musgrove as she was being to her.

Again she thought it would be a mistake.

Instead she said,

"Lodgings in London are very expensive."

"Then I suggest is that you look harder," Lady Musgrove retorted. "I am sure in some back alley you will find a cheap bedroom where, at least, you can spend any free time you have, rather than staying here in Grosvenor Square."

As she finished speaking she turned on her heel and swept out of the office.

She shut the door noisily behind her.

'She *is* ghastly,' Dorina thought. 'I expect she is honey-mouthed and charming when the Earl is here. But he has no idea that she can be so poisonous to anyone she thinks is beneath her.'

She did not see Lady Musgrove again and learned later that, after waiting for another hour, she had left.

"Good riddance to bad rubbish, as far as I'm concerned," the butler said.

Dorina laughed.

"She certainly told me off and I expect when she comes back again she will hope to find this room empty."

"Don't take any notice what she says to you," Henly told her. "She's been the same ever since I first saw her. She orders me about and complains that the food isn't cooked as she really likes it. Then when his Lordship appears she's sweetness and light."

"Does he believe all that nonsense?" Dorina asked.

Henly shrugged his shoulders.

"Men are always taken in by a pretty face," he replied. "Her Ladyship never lets him forget for a moment that she was once known as the prettiest girl in Mayfair."

"I'm surprised at that!" Dorina exclaimed with unusual tartness.

The butler grinned in comprehension.

"That was ten years ago," he told her. "Now I think her looks have got as sharp as her tongue, and that's saying something!"

Dorina laughed.

"It certainly is," she agreed. "I only hope that his Lordship does not listen to her. But I suppose all men like to be praised."

The butler thought for a moment before saying,

"If a man has any sense he'd want to see the woman

he marries when she's her real self and not blinding him from the truth, which he learns soon enough after they are married."

"Now you're being very cynical," Dorina said.

"When you work for an Earl you do get a bit cynical about the tricks ladies get up to," he said. "They all want to trap him into marriage. She's not the only one."

"No, I'm sure." Dorina agreed, thinking of Elsie.

'How can they do it?' she thought silently. 'How can any woman marry a man for his title? When I marry, if I ever do, I want to be very much in love.'

The butler left her and sometime later she heard the Earl's voice in the hall and knew that he had returned.

To her surprise, for it was something he had not done before, he came into her office instead of sending for her to go to his sitting room.

"How were the races?" she asked, thinking how well he looked.

"Wonderful. My horse won. Now I'm in festive mood, and want to celebrate. Let us go out somewhere tonight."

"What?" she echoed, half laughing.

"Come, let us have an evening of celebration. We will wine, dine and be merry. Say that you'll come with me."

"Yes, of course" she replied, laughing openly now, with sheer delight at the thought of an evening with him.

"Let me tell you – " he began.

But before he could say any more they heard the butler's step outside. The next moment he entered with a letter on a silver salver.

"This has just been delivered, my Lord," he said, "and the bearer of it is waiting for an answer."

The Earl picked up the letter.

As he looked at the writing, Dorina thought a frown appeared between his eyes.

He opened the letter, read its contents and then said to the butler.

"Tell the bearer that I will send an answer tomorrow," he said, almost curtly.

"Very good, my Lord," the butler replied and left the room.

The Earl looked at the letter again for a moment and then put it aside. Dorina stared at him. She was almost certain that the letter had come from Lady Musgrove.

Now he said,

"Splendid. That's settled. We'll have dinner together tonight, and go on with the discussion we were enjoying. There's so much more I want to tell you."

But the door opened and the butler entered again.

"Lady Musgrove is here to see you, my Lord."

The Earl looked up in surprise. Lady Musgrove appeared looking, Dorina noticed, even smarter and more elegant than she had looked when she called before.

"Gerald!" she exclaimed. "I thought we were having luncheon together."

At the same time she held out both her hands towards him.

He rose from the chair and took one of her hands in his saying as he did so,

"This is a surprise. I have only just returned home and I thought, if you hadn't heard from me, you would understand that it was impossible for me to have luncheon with you yesterday."

"But I wanted you to have luncheon with me," she said with an attempt at winsomeness, "as it was my birthday, and you promised a long time ago to spend the day with me."

Dorina knew by the expression on the Earl's face that he had forgotten.

Because she knew it was embarrassing, she slipped out of her chair and walked towards the door.

Even before she reached it, Lady Musgrove was saying,

"How could you have forgotten? I've been counting the days to when we would be together and when we would celebrate what is to me an important occasion."

"I'm sorry, I can only apologise," the Earl was saying as Dorina shut the door.

As she walked towards the office she could not help hoping that he was not deceived by such a woman.

'But suppose he is,' she thought. 'Perhaps he will take her out tonight, instead of me.'

The thought caused a little stab of disappointment in her breast. As Miss Radford she would have been immune from such careless treatment, but as a mere secretary she must learn to accept it.

But she was mostly concerned on his behalf, she told herself firmly. She would be sorry to see such an otherwise admirable man behave so shabbily.

Her disappointment at not sharing an evening with him was nothing to do with it.

Absolutely nothing.

But in a short time she heard the front door open and Lady Musgrove, still talking, depart through it.

After a moment she heard footsteps approaching and Henly looked in to say,

"His Lordship's asked me to tell you to be ready in an hour's time."

Her heart singing, Dorina hurried up to her bedroom.

Celia was there to help her and she gasped as they

went through her wardrobe.

"Oh miss, they're so lovely. This pink one – "

"Yes," Dorina said. "I think I'll wear that."

It did not fit with her pose as a secretary, she realised, but then none of her clothes did. It came from Lentheric in Paris and was damask, heavily adorned. The low neck was trimmed with tulle and lace, and the festoons clung deliciously round the hem. It was magnificent.

The Earl was waiting for her at the bottom of the stairs, splendidly dressed for the evening. He bowed when he saw her and led her out to the waiting carriage.

As Dorina stepped into it, she thought that nothing would infuriate Lady Musgrove more than if she knew the common secretary to whom she had been so rude, was being taken out by the Earl instead of herself.

It was however something she could not say.

Instead she persuaded the Earl to talk about the races and how he had felt when his horse won.

"The moment I saw that horse at Tattersall's," he said, "I knew it was a winner, although everyone told me it looked too thin and too small."

He laughed as he added,

"Now they'll realise that I'm a judge of horseflesh."

Dorina smiled.

"Every man wants to feel that," she said. "But I'm sure it's the same with a horse as with anything else – when you see a winner you recognise it with your heart rather than your eyes."

The Earl laughed.

Then he said,

"I think that applies also to what we feel when we meet a lovely woman like yourself. I realise now that you disguise your looks and your golden hair when you are playing the part of a secretary. But now I can see you as you really are."

"How can you be sure of that?" Dorina asked.

"Because I am looking at you not only with my eyes but with something more perceptive," the Earl said.

"I wonder if that is true?" Dorina questioned.

"I think when you are older and have seen as much of the world as I have," the Earl replied, "you will realise that you see people, perhaps, with your heart rather than with your eyes."

"If that's true, then you will not make so many mistakes," Dorina answered. "It's very difficult to sum up another person, especially when they are doing their best to please you."

She was thinking of Lady Musgrove as she spoke.

The Earl was silent for a moment, then he said,

"I've never concealed the fact that I'm suspicious of you. You're not who you pretend to be."

He let a silence fall, as though he was expecting her to say something. But Dorina merely smiled at him. She felt happy and completely mistress of the situation.

The other women could gnash their teeth. He had chosen to be here with her.

He smiled back, completely understanding her silence. It was as though she had thrown a gauntlet down between them.

"I expect," he said, "that one day I will be able to find out if what I am feeling is the truth."

"And what are you feeling?" she asked innocently.

But he shook his head.

"We'll soon be at our destination," he said. "So, what we feel is something we'll have to talk about another time."

"Another time," she whispered, gazing at him in the semi-darkness.

"Yes. It will be something to look forward to. Now, let us think only of enjoying ourselves."

"Where are we going?"

"To the Royal Alhambra Palace. Have you ever heard of it?"

"I think so," she said slowly, wondering if the stories that had reached her could really be true. If so it was a strange destination for a gentleman to take a lady.

It was rumoured to be very thrilling in a manner that was 'not quite proper'. Young men and women flirted outrageously in an atmosphere of freedom and merriment.

"The place is notorious," a starched matron had once told Dorina.

"But I understand that families go there," she had protested. "Husbands and wives take their children there to see the performances."

"To be sure there is a 'family section'," the matron conceded. "And respectable people sit in it. But this is a mere fig-leaf to hide the impropriety. The fact is – " she lowered her voice dramatically, "women are permitted to enter *alone.*"

"Alone?"

"Without a male escort. Any woman can approach the ticket office and obtain entrance *alone.* And, of course, many women do, because it is there that they find the unattached male company that they seek. What this does for the moral tone, I need not describe."

And this was the establishment to which the Earl was taking her?

At last the carriage drew up in Leicester Square, and at once Dorina knew that this was not the kind of place she had ever seen before. It was a huge building, five storeys high, painted a cream colour and adorned with minarets and turrets in a manner clearly meant to suggest the East.

The way in was along a passage that was already crowded with men and women. At last they came to a hole in the wall, behind which sat a young man at a desk. He glanced up briefly, but at the sight of the Earl his face lit up in a smile.

"Evening, sir. Nice to see you. Two?"

Dorina had the feeling that the Earl was displeased at this sign of recognition. His voice was slightly tense as he said,

"Yes, please."

He handed over two shillings and received in return two circular pieces of tin, each with a hole in the centre and inscribed with raised lettering.

A little further on they came to a door, guarded by a man in a red uniform, his breast adorned with medals. He, too, seemed to recognise the Earl, for he grinned at him in a knowing way before allowing his eyes to flicker over Dorina.

It seemed to her that he regarded her with appreciation and she began to feel a little indignant.

They entered a huge rotunda, nearly a hundred feet across and the same in height. Looking up to the ceiling, Dorina saw tier after tier filled with people enjoying themselves in various stages of merriment.

The performance had already begun. A troupe of ballet girls was prancing lightly around the stage, showing much leg and receiving much appreciation from noisy young men.

Dorina stared, remembering the starched matron's warnings, which seemed to be true.

Looking around, she saw the centre of the ground floor, which had been railed off. Here were seated what appeared to be families, husbands, wives, young people.

This must be the family section that was no more than a 'fig-leaf for impropriety'.

The Earl led her to one of the front stalls. Plainly this part of the house was respectable.

But the rest was as far from respectable as Dorina had ever seen.

She was puzzled. Something very strange seemed to be going on.

CHAPTER FIVE

Dorina stared around trying to take in everything about the Alhambra.

Young men with hot eyes prowled about in search of young women, of whom there were plenty. Everywhere there seemed to be bars with liquor dispensed by pretty young bar-maids. Champagne flowed and the air was full of raucous laughter.

The ballet came to an end amid much applause.

Dorina thought of her mother, and knew she would have been shocked to see her here. How could the Earl have done this?

But then she realised that he saw her, not as an unchaperoned young lady, but as someone who would find the somewhat risqué atmosphere acceptable.

'I suppose he thinks that, because I go out to work, and manage without a chaperone, and sleep in his house, therefore I'm a woman of the world,' she mused. 'If only he knew how far from the truth that is. I suppose Lady Musgrove would love it.'

She found the thought vaguely disturbing. She did not want to be put on the same level as Lady Musgrove, whom she considered a thoroughly vulgar woman despite her title.

And what about 'Elsie' who had written him a passionate letter, saying how she remembered 'that magical evening'? Why had it been magical? Where had they been? Here?

How many women had he brought to this place?

Was she merely the latest in a long line? Did he bring respectable ladies here, tantalising them with the promise of an excitement outside their normal experience? 'Just a little bit naughty, but not too much.' And then what?

She turned and found the Earl looking at her, admiration in his eyes.

"My Lord – " she began.

"Why don't you call me Gerald?" he said.

The words caught her off-guard.

"I hardly like to," she demurred. "I am your secretary, almost your servant – "

"Certainly not. Tonight we are two friends enjoying each other's company. Gerald and – Dorina?"

"Dorina," she agreed.

There was a laugh from behind them. Looking back, Dorina saw a little group of people who were undoubtedly a family. The sight reassured her. Whatever was happening in the rest of the Alhambra, there was a respectable part.

The next ballet started. It was vaguely about sea nymphs, which gave all the ballet girls an excuse to dress very lightly in floating, semi-transparent costumes. Dorina found herself blushing.

Then she came to a decision. She prided herself on being a strong woman who could grasp a situation and deal with it.

Very well, then.

As the music ended she joined in the applause as though she had not a care in the world. She smiled at the Earl and said,

"I feel rather thirsty. Perhaps we could walk about and

find one of those bars, where we can have something to drink?"

He was instantly uneasy.

"I don't think that would be a very good idea," he demurred. "Perhaps we should leave and find a restaurant?

"Oh no, I want to see the next ballet," she said implacably. "That gives us half an hour to go to one of the bars."

His uneasiness grew.

"I don't think you'd like the kind of people you'd meet there," he said.

Dorina gave a laugh which she hoped sounded naïve and foolish.

"But of course I shall. After all, you brought me here. I know that you wouldn't bring me anywhere unsuitable. Why don't we go now?"

She rose determinedly and began to make her way along the row of stalls. At the end she turned, so that she was facing the exit from the railed-off 'respectable' area. Once past that rail, there was no knowing what might happen.

His hand on her arm detained her.

"I think it's best if we leave," he said firmly.

"Kennington! Hey there old fellow!"

He turned in answer to a shout from a man he recognised as an old friend. In fact they had seen each other earlier at the races.

"Harris," he said, trying to sound genial yet edging away as he spoke.

"Spending your winnings, old fellow?" Harris said knowingly. "Don't blame you."

"Yes, it was a good day out," the Earl agreed, "but if you don't mind – "

But Harris, a large, moustachioed man, was impervious to hints.

"Very attractive filly of yours. Went like the wind. So now you're celebrating with another little filly, eh? Very nice too."

The Earl's voice became frozen.

"She is a lady – "

"Of course she is. They always are old boy, until you've spent enough."

Appalled the Earl turned to see if Dorina could hear any of this.

But she was not there.

The chance to slip away had been too good to lose. In seconds Dorina was lost in the crowd, seizing the chance to look around her.

At first glance the revelry was simply bright and cheerful. Here was a bar and just along there was another one, piled high with brightly coloured bottles.

All around her were young women dressed almost as well as herself. Their gowns were fashionable and elegantly decorated. They seemed confident and assured, making eyes at the men and laughing with them, seemingly on equal terms. These were women of independence.

But a closer look revealed the tense looks in their eyes. It was imperative to them to attract the attention of men with money to spend. That was how they survived.

What saddened Dorina most was the fact that not all of them were openly vulgar. Some looked as though they might have been ladies, who knew about fine living and elegant manners.

Someone collided with her. Two big hands seized her bare arms to steady her and a tipsy voice said,

"Not to worry, my dear. I've got you safe."

"Let me go," she said, trying to pull away.

But the hands held her tightly.

"All in good time. After all, *you* bumped into *me.*"

"That was an accident," she protested.

"Oh, I don't think so. There's accidents and accidents, and I know the difference. You chose me, and you made a good choice. See this?"

He removed one hand and pointed to a glittering bauble on the front of his shirt.

"Real diamonds," he said. "But of course you knew that."

In fact a quick glance had been enough to tell Dorina that the diamonds were fake. She wondered how many women he had fooled that way. Or was he fooled himself?

"Now, why don't we go and enjoy ourselves?" he sniggered, breathing whisky fumes all over her.

With a huge effort Dorina put her hands on his chest and gave an almighty shove, strong enough to send him backwards. When he tried to lunge towards her again she turned on him, eyes glittering and finger pointing.

"Don't," she hissed.

He backed off at once, alarmed by something he had seen in her eyes. He could not have said exactly what, but he felt mysteriously afraid.

Dorina tried to hurry away from him, but in the tightly-packed crowd she could not move far, and she was able to overhear a conversation between two other men who had witnessed the little scene and enjoyed it.

"You can't blame him for trying," one observed. "But he lacks the style to lure a really prime article."

"And she certainly is a prime article," the other one agreed.

"She might almost be a lady," said the first man.

"Perhaps she is a lady?"

"Not in this part of the house, old fellow. But you've got to admit, she's more convincing than most."

Trembling with rage, Dorina stood frozen, listening to every word.

"Now just watch her," the first man said. "She'll look around and pick out a man she thinks looks wealthy enough to satisfy her. Then she'll slip her arm through his and say, "would you care to buy me a drink, sir?"

"Oh, will she?" Dorina muttered.

"Look, there's a fellow coming close behind her now," said the man. "He looks as if he could afford the earth, so he'll do for her. There he goes."

At that very moment a hand touched Dorina's arm from behind. Without a second's thought she swung round and delivered a punch of which a boxer would have been proud.

She heard screams and commotion as her victim fell to the ground. Furiously she stood over him, ready to deliver another punch if he dared to get up.

Then she froze.

"Gerald!"

He was lying on the floor, his eyes closed, and she could not tell if he was conscious or not. But before she could drop down beside him, she felt yet another hand seize her. It was heavy, and it landed on her shoulder.

"That's enough," said the policeman. "You know the terms on which we allow you girls in here. No rough stuff. I'm arresting you – "

"But I'm not one of those women," she cried.

"That's what they all say. Come along."

Against her will she was being hauled away, and there was nothing she could do about it.

"Gerald!" she screamed.

But he lay on the floor, his eyes still closed, unable to help her.

Heads turned as the policemen dragged her struggling figure out of the Alhambra. She managed to land a good few kicks on his shins, but not to escape him.

"Now then, now then," he said. "We don't want to add assaulting a police officer to the other charges, do we?"

"What other charges?" she gasped in horror.

"Don't give me that. You know what the charges are. You've probably been this way a dozen times for all you look like butter wouldn't melt in your mouth. When we get to the station I expect we'll find you have quite a record."

By now he had got her outside, where a police van was waiting.

"In you go," he said, pulling open a door with a barred window at the back, and letting down the steps.

Despite her struggles, Dorina found herself shoved into the van. The door was slammed, and the next thing she knew, she was on the move. She flung herself against the door, but it was locked. All she could do was stare frantically through the bars at the retreating street.

"Don't worry, love," said a voice behind her. "You'll get used to it like we all do."

Aghast, Dorina turned and saw what she had not noticed before.

There were five other women in there with her, some of whom, as the woman had said, looked as though they had indeed been through this many times before.

She was a prisoner on her way to a Police Station to be charged with any number of unmentionable crimes.

And there was nobody to help her.

*

When his head cleared, the Earl found himself sitting on the floor, leaning against a pillar. Gingerly he felt his jaw.

"What happened?" he mumbled.

"You had a lucky escape," said a male voice above him. "She may look like an angel but she's got a punch like a prize fighter."

Things began to come back to the Earl and he groaned. Hands reached out to help him into a chair.

"I remember now," he said. "Poor girl."

"Poor girl," said another male voice. "She knocked you out."

"She did not," he said, stung. "She caught me off guard. I lost my balance and hit my head on the pillar."

"That's not what the charge sheet will say," someone observed, and there was a burst of laughter.

"What do you mean, charge sheet?" the Earl demanded in alarm.

"The law dealt with her. There's always the odd policeman here to make sure that the girls behave themselves, and arrest them when they don't. He saw what happened and took her off."

"Oh no!" the Earl groaned, hiding his face in his hands. "Please tell me you didn't really say that."

"Don't worry, old boy. The police won't make you appear in court. They don't like to do that because it embarrasses a fellow – if he happens to have a wife or something like that. And the officer saw her assault you, so they won't need your testimony. So you can afford to forget about her."

The Earl groaned again.

"Where is she?" he demanded. "Where did they take her?"

"Don't go following her. Let her go. It's best if you

never see her again."

"Where will she be?" he shouted.

"They take them to the Haymarket Police Station, just round the corner," the man said. "But if you'll take my advice, you'll leave her to her fate."

Shocked to the soul by this catastrophe, the Earl forced himself to rise and make his way out of the Alhambra. His head was still swimming from where it had struck the pillar and his jaw was sore.

He felt it gingerly.

'Who would have thought she could do that?' he mused. 'But it was all my own fault. Whatever can I say to her after this?'

All too soon the Police Station came in sight. As soon as he appeared in the doorway, the sergeant at the desk stood up straight and alert, awed by the Earl's elegant evening wear. He was dealing with 'quality'.

Overcoming his embarrassment as best he could, the Earl told a pathetic and not entirely untruthful story about taking a lady friend to the Alhambra, losing track of her, and then falling victim to her wrath.

"She is not – the kind of woman you think," he said. "The fault was mine for taking a well bred lady to such a place."

"I don't know about a well bred lady," the desk sergeant protested. "From what I heard she has a splendid right hook."

The Earl ground his teeth.

"I slipped," he said tensely. "And banged my head. Besides, you can hardly blame the poor girl for being angry with me."

The sergeant became fatherly.

"Now look here, sir, I understand that you feel a sense

of responsibility for this young person – "

"This young *lady*," the Earl corrected him with an edge to his voice.

"If you say so, sir."

"I do say so, and since I am the Earl of Kennington, the correct way for you to address me is 'my Lord'."

Normally he was the last person to emphasise his title, but he could see that he was going to need all the status he could summon. Luckily this produced the desired result, at least in part. The sergeant became more respectful, but no less avuncular.

"Yes my Lord," he said. "I'm sure it's very good of you to be so concerned about her, but there's no need to go worrying too much. These girls know how to take care of themselves – "

In despair, the Earl played his highest card.

"The young lady happens to be my fiancée," he said in a freezing voice.

"Really, sir? Then you'll be able to tell me her name."

"Hasn't she already told you?"

"No, my Lord, she's been extremely unhelpful and refused to utter a word."

"Then I'm certainly not going to tell you. But what I will say is this. If you are so misguided as to take this lady to court I shall appear before the magistrate, making it plain that I have no charges to press against her. I shall get the best solicitor I can find to defend her, and then I shall bring an action against the police for false arrest, imprisonment and malicious prosecution."

The sergeant knew when he was beaten.

"In that case, my Lord, I'll have the young lady brought up from the cells to be released. Then the two of you can sort it out any way you can."

The Earl sat gloomily watching the door. The waiting was terrible, but he knew that the moment when Dorina appeared would be far worse.

He wondered if she would be tearful or reproachful. If he was very lucky indeed she might even be apologetic for the injury she had inflicted on him.

But he did not count on his luck to extend that far.

As soon as he saw her he knew that he had been right. Nothing prepared him for the avenging fury that appeared and fixed baleful eyes on him. Dorina's hair was dishevelled, her eyes wild, and she regarded the Earl with a fierce hostility that boded ill for him.

"If you'll just sign here, saying that you do not wish to press charges of assault – " said the sergeant.

The Earl signed hurriedly.

"Good. Now you can take your fiancée with you."

At the words 'your fiancée' Dorina's rage nearly boiled over. The Earl hastily grasped her arm and whisked her out of the door before she could make anything worse.

"Goodnight," he called hurriedly over his shoulder.

"Goodnight, my Lord," the sergeant replied, adding under his breath,

"And I wouldn't be in your shoes for all the tea in China."

"Not a word," the Earl told her when they were in the street. "You can say it all to me when we get home."

"I never wish to speak to you again," she told him bitterly. "Not when we get home, not tomorrow, not ever. As far as I'm concerned *you do not exist*."

Unwisely he attempted to joke.

"Well, somebody nearly dislocated my jaw."

"Would you like me to do it properly?" she flashed.

"Look there's a cab," he said, hastily, waving with relief to an approaching vehicle.

They got in and sat side by side for the journey to Grosvenor Square. Now and then the Earl turned his head to look at Dorina, but she sat, stony-faced, staring into space, refusing to give him so much as a glance.

"I only want you to know that I'm sorry," he said.

Silence. In the dim light he could just see her set her chin a little more firmly.

"It was all my fault, the whole thing."

Silence.

After a journey that seemed to take forever they finally reached his home. It was the Earl's habit to tell his staff not to wait up for him if he was going to be late. Now, he saw with relief that the house was in darkness, save for the light that was left on in the hall. At least they would have privacy for the volcanic quarrel that was about to ensue.

Once the front door was closed behind them, Dorina headed for the stairs, but he stopped her.

"We must talk about this first, Dorina."

"I have nothing to say."

"Well, I have. Surely you can at least listen while I apologise?"

He drew her into the library, closed the door firmly behind them and lit one of the low table lamps. It provided a very imperfect light, but in the dramatic shadows, with her eyes flashing, he thought she looked magnificent.

"Apologise?" she said fiercely. "Do you think any apology can make up for what you did to me?"

"What I – ? Wait a moment, *you* punched *me,* when there was no need."

"There was every need. I shall always be glad to remember that I knocked you off your feet."

"I slipped," he said tensely. "You caught me by surprise."

"Surprise? You were surprised that I rounded on you after you dared to take me to that – that – ?"

"The Alhambra is a theatre, and like all theatres it gets less salubrious the higher you go. Ladies know to stay in the stalls, where they're safe."

"Are you saying that I'm not a lady?" she flung at him.

He drew a sharp breath. This was going dreadfully wrong. He wanted to throw himself at her feet and beg her forgiveness. He wanted to take her in his arms and promise to care for her forever. But it was turning into a quarrel.

"Please, Dorina, I didn't mean – "

"You will address me as Miss Martin, when you address me at all, which won't be for much longer. And don't talk nonsense about the Alhambra being like other theatres, because it definitely is not – which you must have known perfectly well."

"It's a little more extreme than some," he agreed, "but it's still a place where a respectable man can take a respectable woman, as long as she observes the boundaries."

"And just what are your boundaries, my Lord?" Dorina asked in a dangerous voice.

"I don't know what you mean."

"I think you do. You have a dividing line in your mind, don't you? On one side are the ladies of delicate sensibilities whose virtue must be protected, and whom you would never dream of taking to the Alhambra.

"On the other side there are the women of the world, respectable but rather more knowing. Women like Lady Musgrove, and Elsie – and *me*."

"Dorina – Miss Martin – "

"Lady Musgrove," Dorina went on remorselessly. "A

woman of so little delicacy that she pursues you to your home as no lady would ever do. But perhaps I shouldn't blame her, since you must have given her some cause for such confidence.

"And the same goes for Elsie, who writes you such passionate letters. Again, no doubt she feels she has reason. Just as you must feel you have reason to show them so little respect.

"But me? What excuse have I given you to insult me? I'm a working woman and have to live in the world. I have no father or brothers to protect me. Is that reason enough? Yes, I suppose it would be for a hardened womaniser."

"I don't think that's very – "

"I had not finished speaking," Dorina informed him in arctic tones.

"Then kindly don't call me a hardened womaniser."

"After the insults you have offered me tonight, I consider it a fairly mild return," she seethed.

"I never meant to insult you, and if you think I'm a hardened womaniser, all I can is that you've never known one. And if it's an insult for me to call you my fiancée – "

"That was the worst," Dorina declared on a sob. "And if you think that I should be flattered, then let me make it plain to you that *I would sooner proclaim my betrothal to a python."*

Shocked, they stared at each other.

The Earl recovered first.

"Thank you," he snapped. "You have made yourself perfectly plain, although why a python I do not understand."

"It was the worst thing I could think of," Dorina said bitterly. "You had no right to say any such thing about me, without my consent."

"I was trying to impress that policeman with your

status, because he thought you were a – a – "

"*I know what he thought I was.* I understood exactly what the police thought when they hauled me away in a van along with five other women. The others thought it terribly funny. They said I'd get used to it in time – "

Her voice broke and a wail came from her. She had kept up a fighting front until now, but suddenly her courage ran out and she sat down on the sofa, burying her face in her hands and sobbing as though her heart would break.

Aghast, the Earl flung himself on his knees beside her.

"Please, please Dorina, I'm sorry. Please don't cry. It was entirely my fault."

He tried to take her into his arms but she threw him off.

"Don't touch me," she wept. "I shall never forgive you for tonight as long as I live."

"And I don't deserve to be forgiven. I should never have taken you there, but I merely thought you'd enjoy a little forbidden excitement like – "

He was going to say, 'like other women I've known' but stopped himself in time. Dorina had been right in saying that Elsie and Lady Musgrove enjoyed going to the Alhambra, where they could burn their fingers just a little, then retreat in safety.

But he saw now that he should never have confused Dorina with such creatures who, for all their titles and aristocratic pretensions, had much in common with the good-time girls of the Alhambra.

"I was wrong, terribly wrong," he said, shame-faced. "But please, darling, say you'll forgive me, and we can start again."

"Don't call me darling," she sobbed. "And we can't start again. I'm going away."

"No, you mustn't leave. I want to make things right."

She shook her head in vigorous denial, but he would not accept it. Her hands were still covering her face and he gently reached up and drew them down.

"It was all my fault," he whispered. "I'll never forgive myself – even if you can find it in your heart to forgive me."

"I can't," she said huskily. "I'll never, never forget tonight."

Distraught, he did not know what to say. He only knew that the sight of her with her hair falling about her shoulders, tears streaming down her face, affected him as nothing ever had in his life before.

"Dorina," he whispered, "Dorina – "

But her sobs did not cease, and comforting her became the most important thing in the world.

Forgetting everything except the bewildering sensation in his heart, he reached out to put his arms round her, pulling her against him.

The next moment his lips found hers.

CHAPTER SIX

Dorina was stunned. At one moment she was in the depths of despair. The next she seemed to be transported into a new realm, full of starlight.

A number of men had kissed her cheek after they had had an enjoyable dance. But she had never been kissed on the lips before.

As the Earl's lips held hers captive, she felt something very strange within her heart, something different from anything she had ever felt before.

She wondered how such a sensation could exist without her discovering it until now. It seemed to fill all the world.

She was possessed by a strange sweet feeling, warm and exciting. She wanted this closeness to go on forever. She longed to be even closer to him, lips to lips and heart to heart.

She began to reach for him, meaning to put her arms about him.

But something stopped her.

It was as though a cold hand had descended on her shoulder, warning her to pull back, reminding her how easily he did this, how practised he seemed.

At all costs she must stop now, this minute.

Images of the Alhambra swirled through her head. Those young women she had seen tonight, with careless manners and fashionable clothes so like her own!

Why had he taken her to that risqué place? Was it to break down her defences and create the right mood for seduction?

"No," she cried, struggling free. "No, let me go."

"I'll never let you go," he said hoarsely. "Please Dorina, let's put this behind us. There's so much I – "

But she freed herself and ran to the door.

"Don't talk to me," she cried. "Don't try to find me. Don't even think of me again."

In her mind was the torturing memory of how nearly she had succumbed to his embrace only a few moments ago. She hated and despised him, yet his kiss – cynical though she knew it to be – had sent her into ecstasies.

She was horrified at herself. After this she would go right away and never again think of anything but piston engines. At least in them she would find safety.

The Earl watched her in despair. Just at the moment when he had begun to understand how vital she was to him, he was losing her forever. He reached for her again, but she thrust him away.

Her arms were made strong by desperation and her push was hard enough to send him back hard against the door jamb. He let out a groan as the wood struck his head at exactly the same point where he'd received the earlier blow.

"Ouch!" he cried.

Dorina froze.

"What is it?" she asked, trying not to sound as anxious as she felt.

"Nothing, I – "

Suddenly the Earl fell silent as he realised how close

he had come to throwing away his best chance.

"It – it's nothing," he said quickly. "Just my head."

"You hardly banged your head at all," she said, suspicious, but not moving away from him.

"Not this time, but before – when you punched me to the floor at the Alhambra. I hit my head on the pillar and it knocked me out for a moment. But it's all right now."

He finished with a melancholy groan and sat down, holding his head.

"I didn't mean to hurt you," she said in a faltering voice. "Besides, I didn't punch you to the floor. You slipped. You said so."

"That's right, I did. It was my own fault. Don't worry about me."

She dropped down beside him, frowning and saying uneasily,

"I don't like to think of you being really hurt."

"I thought that was what you wanted."

"Of course not. I just – I'm sending for the doctor."

"I don't want to trouble him," he said bravely.

"But you can't take any chances," Dorina cried. "You might have a terrible injury to your head. I didn't mean any of those things I said – well, I did, but – oh, I don't know what I'm saying."

"It doesn't matter now. I'm sorry about everything. I'll just go up to bed. Perhaps – perhaps you could help me."

She shot him a quick look, full of renewed suspicion. His eyes met hers, as innocent as a baby's.

"I do not trust you, my Lord," Dorina said slowly.

"How can you not trust me?" he complained. "You nearly killed me."

"I *should* have done."

"You're a heartless woman."

A faint smile touched her lips, but she suppressed it instantly.

"Let me help you," she offered.

She was forced to let him slip an arm around her shoulders as they made their way slowly upstairs as far as his door. There was something strangely sweet about the feel of his weight, half leaning on her.

She was uncertain what to believe. She had been shocked at herself for throwing a punch at him in the Alhambra, and even more shocked at his fall, although she had realised even then that it had been mostly accidental.

She knew he had struck his head, and had been dazed for long enough for her to be hauled away. But how serious was it? She was no fool. It was clear that he had thrown himself on her mercy now, as a way of keeping her here. He was hardly pretending otherwise. But behind the pretence, might he not really be hurt?

On the landing she saw two shadowy figures, and was relieved to recognise Blake, the Earl's valet and the butler, both in their dressing gowns, summoned by the strange noises they had heard below.

"Is something wrong, my Lord?" Blake asked anxiously.

"Yes, his Lordship needs a doctor," Dorina said. "He has been set upon by footpads and viciously clubbed half to death."

"No, that was just in your wishful dreams," the Earl murmured in her ear.

"Be silent," she told him firmly, handing him over to the valet, while the butler went about summoning the doctor.

At the last moment the Earl tightened his hand on her arm.

"You won't go?" he asked, and, although his tone was light, the anxiety in his eyes was real.

"Not until the doctor tells me you are well."

She hurried away to her own room, and began to tear off her evening dress, which she knew she would never wear again.

In its place she donned a severe, striped blouse, with a white collar. It had a faintly mannish air, and she wore it when she wanted to be businesslike. When she had buttoned it up to the throat she set to work on her hair, drawing it back firmly against her skull in the grimmest style she could imagine.

She emerged just after the doctor had arrived. Blake informed her in hushed accents that Dr. Jones had just gone into his Lordship's room.

"I put him to bed, miss. He was looking very pale, and groaning a lot."

Inside his bedroom the Earl was still groaning until the doctor said,

"You can stop that. It was just a little bump on the head."

"It's going to do its work very nicely, though," the Earl growled. "I shall need at least a couple of days' perfect rest and careful nursing."

"If you say so," the doctor said, grinning. "Do you want me to notify Lady Musgrove or any other of the – ?"

"No," the Earl said explosively. "All that's over. Things are different now."

"I see," the doctor said, slightly startled by the Earl's forceful tone.

He eyed his patient, his head on one side and mused,

"You used not to have to go to these lengths to secure a woman's interest."

"I don't know what you're talking about," the Earl riposted.

"Don't worry, I'll say all the right things."

Seeing wrath in his patient's eye, the doctor hastened into the corridor where he was met by a young woman of quelling aspect.

"I am his Lordship's secretary," she declared. "How is his Lordship? Is his head seriously hurt?"

"He'll benefit from a few days' quiet rest in bed and careful nursing," the doctor recited obediently. "He can see any visitors that he pleases. I'm sure I can entrust him into your capable hands."

As he departed, the doctor wondered who was the lady whom the Earl was trying to attract. Doubtless she was the kind of voluptuous, melting creature that he had often chosen in his colourful romantic career. But if she was intending to visit his sick-room, the doctor doubted that she would make much headway against that terrifying secretary.

*

The Earl remained officially an invalid for only one day, rising when he realised that Dorina was determined not to set foot in his room.

On the second morning he confronted her in the office, where she was opening correspondence.

"Thank you for not leaving," he said.

"I promised to remain until your Lordship was recovered," she said primly.

"I'm touched by your concern for my health, although it did not lead you to visit me."

"There was no need," she said, without looking up. "Your valet was able to do all that was necessary."

With dismay he saw that she was dressed to repel, in her plain blouse, her hair sleeked back severely. The sight told him that he had not been forgiven, and must tread carefully.

"Let us look at the correspondence," he said, taking his cue from her.

"There are some letters here that need your immediate attention – "

She pushed them over to him and they settled down to work. He dictated replies until he could endure the atmosphere no longer, then he rose, saying,

"I'm afraid I've piled rather a lot on to you. Will you be able to finish it all today?"

If she had said, 'easily,' he would have given her more. He dreaded that she might slip away.

But she said,

"I may not get through all of it – "

"Well, you can finish it off tomorrow. I'm going out now. When I return you can tell me about any problems that may have arisen."

"I will do so, my Lord."

She did not look up, and after a moment he departed.

When she heard the front door close behind him, Dorina let her shoulders sag. She had been full of tension the whole time he had been there, knowing that she ought to leave this house, yet mysteriously unable to tear herself away.

Could any man be worth what she had endured the other night?

'My work is worth it,' she told herself. 'I must stay to learn more.'

But then she remembered the tone of his voice as he had begged her forgiveness, and the feel of his lips on hers, and she knew that the real reason had nothing to do with work.

In the early evening the Earl arrived home in a state of high excitement. He came straight to Dorina's office, his eyes shining.

"Whatever has happened?" she asked, almost laughing as she saw his face.

"I've been to one of my factories in another part of London and I have wonderful news."

"Tell me," she said eagerly.

"Recently you were asking me about the horseless carriage and I put you off. Well, now I can tell you that I have made a big step forward."

Dorina gasped. To him this was a wonderful development, but she was torn two ways. She wanted his success, but she also wanted her own.

"We're going to be the first," he said, seizing her hands eagerly. "Imagine that! It's a revolution, and we will be at the forefront, leading the world."

"But – the other night you were talking as though it was a long time in the future."

"I know. I was confused. I didn't dare let myself hope and talking about it seemed like bad luck. But now – now, I think I can hope, and the first person I wanted to tell was you. Do you understand why?"

"Yes," she said slowly. "I think I do."

She was pulled this way and that between joy and despair. He wanted to draw close to her, as close as she wanted to be with him. At the same time he threatened her greatest hopes. And he also made her realise how terrible it was that she could not be honest with him.

Where did her loyalties lie? With her father's firm, of that she was sure. It had to be so.

Yet this man could make her feel that nothing mattered but to be with him.

He seemed to become aware that he was still holding her hands, and dropped them, suddenly self-conscious.

"I want you to come with me now, and see my invention for yourself," he said, "because you are the only person who can fully understand. You have to see it, because if I describe it you won't believe it.

"And I want to tell you everything, from the very beginning, how this has been planned and how my ideas have grown until now they are on the verge of success. Will you come with me?"

"Of course I will," she cried joyfully.

"Then quickly put on your hat and coat, and off we go."

Everything was happening in such a whirl that she had no time to think. It wasn't until they were in the carriage and moving away fast that she knew a qualm of conscience.

"Are you sure about confiding so much in me?" she asked. "If it's new and revolutionary, it might make your fortune."

"I hope it will."

"But don't you see, there must be other people trying to create the same thing. If a great new invention is 'in the air', then several people will think of it at once, because its time has come."

He looked at her curiously.

"How strange that you should say that," he mused. "It's true, of course, but not many people know it. You must know more about this business than I ever dreamed."

"I – I was quoting someone," she stammered.

She had been quoting her father, but she could not say that.

"Are you going to tell me who?"

"No," she said firmly. "I merely want to warn you

about telling me too much about your miracle. How do you know that I'm not a spy from another camp? You've said yourself that I'm strangely well informed."

The Earl laughed. "Why are you trying to make me think ill of you? Whoever you are, wherever you come from, I know that I can trust you."

"Forgive me, my Lord, but you know no such thing."

"But I do. Now, I don't want to hear any more. We shall soon be reaching the factory. It's situated in rather a rough district, but don't be worried. No harm will come to you."

Looking out of the window she could see that he was right. The streets were becoming dingy and poor, although now that the lights were coming on they somehow seemed cheerful. But however rough they were, she was not worried. They reminded her of the places in Birmingham where her father's factories were. And she much preferred this honest shabbiness to the glittering decadence of the Alhambra.

At last they arrived at what looked like a very large shed with wide doors. Light was streaming from inside and several men stood ready to greet them.

The Earl assisted Dorina to descend, and introduced her briefly as his secretary. As she was still dressed to look forbidding, nobody thought this strange.

They entered the great shed, which was lit by electricity and full of machinery. All around her Dorina saw working men in leather aprons. It was like meeting up with old friends, for she had known men just like this when she visited her father.

And there was another thing she recognised, the look of joy and pride on their faces that told a tale of work that had come to fruition, of success too long delayed but finally achieved in the face of all odds. It was a look of sheer blazing triumph.

The same look was on the Earl's face.

"Now, are you ready for what I'm going to show you?" he asked.

"I'm quite ready."

"No, you're not. Nobody in the world is ready for this. A carriage that runs by itself without any horses. They said it couldn't be done, but we proved them wrong. Mike – "

On the word a large man with grey hair stepped aside, indicating a very large object that made Dorina's eyes open wide.

It had four wheels and four seats, but there the similarity to a conventional carriage ended. Instead of the seats being arranged in two rows of two, facing each other, both rows faced the front.

The construction was about eight feet long by five feet wide, and stood six feet above the ground.

"All the energy is generated here," the Earl said, laying his hand on a large metal box in the front, from which protruded a long spoke, with a wheel on the end.

"It's powered by a thick, heavy liquid that we call petrol. It works because it can be set alight. Inside this box the petrol is drawn into the cylinder by the piston, and then compressed. Then a spark sets the petrol alight, which forces it up. When the engine is at full blast it can go as fast as four horses all galloping together."

A murmur went round the men who had gathered around them. Four horse power. Fancy that!

He raised the side of the metal box and Dorina peered inside with real interest.

"But with no horses or reins, how do you make it go where you want?" she asked.

"That's what the wheel is for. I'll show you."

He climbed up into one of the front seats and leaned down, giving her his hand to draw her up beside him. The seat was higher than she had expected, and looking down she had a dizzying feeling of delight and excitement. From up here anything seemed possible.

"Let's start up," the Earl called.

"How do you generate the spark?" she asked.

"Like this," he said, pointing to where a man had positioned himself at the front.

The man thrust a bent spoke into the front and began to turn it. At the third turn the metal box started to hum.

"It's alive," she gasped.

"That's it. It's alive, just as horses are alive. It's a different kind of life, but it's still life."

"But it isn't moving."

"Watch down there."

Following his gaze, she saw how he pressed a pedal near the floor. And then slowly, incredibly, the horseless carriage began to move.

A mighty cheer broke out from all the men. Dorina too felt like cheering.

Carefully the Earl turned the wheel to the left, and the carriage moved in the same direction. Then he turned the wheel to the right and again the carriage responded.

Round the great shed he went with Dorina clinging to his arm in transports of delight.

"Oh it's wonderful!" she cried. "Can I try?"

"You mean – you want to drive it?"

"Yes, please."

He drew to a halt and jumped down to the ground, indicating for her to move over behind the wheel. When he had climbed in the other side he showed her the foot pedal.

The engine was still humming.

"Grasp the wheel and press the pedal gently," he said.

Dorina took a deep breath and pressed down with her foot. The carriage began to glide forward and she almost cried out at the wonderful feeling.

"We're moving," she said ecstatically.

"That's right. Now turn the wheel slowly, that's it – "

But in the same moment she seemed to lose control. The carriage swerved and came to an abrupt halt against a heavy piece of machinery. The jolt sent her sideways straight into the Earl's arms.

At once they were surrounded by men, worriedly examining the carriage.

"Have I damaged it?" she cried.

The man called Mike made a reassuring gesture.

"Not so much as a scratch," he said.

There was another cheer. Dorina realised that the Earl's arms were still around her.

"Shall I take over again?" he asked.

"Yes, I think perhaps you should," she said.

They did another few rounds of the shed before coming to a halt.

"I wanted you to see this," he said. "But now I suppose we must stop."

They bade everyone goodnight, and left the shed in a kind of dream.

All the way home they were quiet, awed by the beautiful thing that had happened. Neither of them could find words, but they both knew that they were glad they had shared the moment.

It was about nine o'clock when they reached the house. Henly greeted them in the hall.

"Cook wasn't sure whether you wanted dinner, my Lord."

"Oh dear, I hope she isn't too angry with me," the Earl said. "Please tell her that anything will do."

In the dining room he poured her a sherry and one for himself. Henly came in just then, stiff with disapproval.

"I could have done that for your Lordship."

"Don't worry about it," the Earl said cheerfully.

Henly began to lay the table.

"I have conveyed your message to cook, my Lord, and she says that she does not serve 'anything', but will provide your Lordship with a proper meal."

He sailed out, the picture of outrage.

Dorina gave a choke. The Earl's eyes met hers, gleaming with merriment. Then they laughed out loud together.

"Poor Henly will never recover from you pouring your own sherry," Dorina said. "It is not what an Earl does."

"Well, I'm not a proper Earl, any more than my father was. I'm just an engineer giving himself airs, but at this moment I wouldn't be anyone else in the world. Wasn't it wonderful as we went round and round, taking those turns – "

"Crashing," she reminded him.

"You'll learn. I'll teach you properly, because something tells me that you can understand about this more than any woman in the world, more than any *person* in the world."

Before he could say more Henly swept in with soup. They maintained a sedate silence as he served them and swept out again.

When the door closed behind him they both relaxed.

"I can't stand this," the Earl said. "I've never been in

such trouble before."

"You'll have to apologise to cook," Dorina warned him.

"I was only trying to be kind and helpful," he complained.

"Servants don't always like that," Dorina said. "They think you're implying that they're not up to the job."

She tasted the soup, which was delicious, and so missed the puzzled look that the Earl gave her.

"I wonder how you knew that," he said.

"Knew what?"

"How do you know so much about servants? You speak as though you were used to armies of them. It's just one more mystery to add to the many mysteries about you. Don't you think it's time you told me everything?"

CHAPTER SEVEN

Tell him everything!

The temptation was great and for a moment Dorina almost yielded to it.

But how could she tell him anything after this evening, when he had revealed his secrets to her? If he knew her true identity, he would put the worst construction on everything. It must wait for another time.

So she only smiled mysteriously and shook her head.

"You're right," he said at once. "I have no business asking, especially after I misjudged you so dreadfully."

"Let us not speak of that," she said quickly.

"But I must speak of it. I meant no harm but I was wrong about everything. To a certain kind of sophisticated lady, the Alhambra is nothing but a good joke."

"You mean like Lady Musgrove, or 'Elsie' or, I dare say, many others."

She had not meant to say the last words, but she was inspired by a sudden spurt of jealousy.

"I give you my word," he said, "that I am not a hardened womaniser – "

"No – of course not – please forget that I said that – I had no right – "

"I admit that I have led a colourful life – perhaps too

colourful – but I am not as bad as you think I am."

"I think nothing, my Lord. Nothing at all."

"Is that your way of telling me that I can never be anything to you?"

"I – I cannot say," she faltered. "Please, let us not speak of it now."

Her heart had leapt at his words, with their hint that he loved her, or might come to love her. But she could not respond to him as she might want to. Too much between them was concealed. Love could only flourish in honesty, and that time had not yet come.

"I'm afraid that you are still offended with me," he said. "After what you suffered that night, I cannot blame you. I can only hope that time will erase the memory and you may truly come to forgive me."

"But I have already forgiven you. It was partly my own fault for wandering off like that."

"None of it was your fault," he said warmly. "I should have known better than to take you there. The thing is – I've become a little careless – you might say that I've lived carelessly. This house has seen too many women like Lady Musgrove, and Elsie, and others, I'm afraid."

"You don't owe me any explanations."

"But I want to make things clear between us. Don't you understand why? No, no, pretend I didn't say that. It's too soon. I only want you to know that all that is over. Such ladies are no longer a part of my life."

For a moment she could not answer. She was afraid that if she spoke her voice would shake with the emotion of the moment. What she was hearing was so wonderful, so full of hope and joy for the future, that she could hardly believe it, desperately though she wanted to.

"I – I am sure you have made the right decision, my

Lord," she said at last. "You will be free to concentrate on your great inventions and see them benefit the whole world. You need no distractions."

"Distractions, yes. That's what those frivolous women are. What I need is a woman who is as passionate about my creations as I am myself."

He did not say more, but his eyes intent on Dorina made it clear that she was the woman he had in mind. She felt as though she were floating in a blissful dream.

But his next words shook her to the soul.

"And it will take all the concentration and all the skill of which I am capable, to defeat John Radford."

There was a slight clatter as Dorina set down her wine glass too quickly, and struck her soup bowl.

"John Radford?" she asked faintly.

"My chief rival and the only one that I fear. You know so much, you must surely have heard of him?"

"I have heard the name," Dorina said cautiously. "I believe he too is an engineer of repute."

"Indeed he is, and a very great man," the Earl agreed with a readiness that warmed her to him. "Whatever major engineering developments there have been this century, he has led them."

"He? Not your father?" Dorina could not resist asking.

He made a humorous face.

"No, Radford was always just a little ahead of my father in ingenuity and inventiveness. Not that I would have admitted that while Papa was alive. He too was a great man in his way and he improved dramatically on many of the ideas that were invented by other people. But he seldom got there first, and it was always his ambition to outdo John Radford.

"The only way he managed it was with his title. He was so proud that they made him an Earl and offered Radford nothing. Mind you, I heard rumours that Radford was offered a title and refused it. I'm only glad my father never knew that. It would have spoiled the victory that meant so much to him.

"Since he died, it has been my ambition to outwit John Radford, on my father's behalf. And now – " a glow seemed to light his face, "now I'm finally within sight of doing it. You can't imagine what that means to me."

"Does it matter so much, being the first?" Dorina asked.

"It's the first man whose name goes down in history," the Earl said simply. "John Radford knows that as well as I do. I suspect that's why he's suddenly gone quiet."

"How do you mean?" Dorina asked in alarm.

"He almost seems to have vanished from the face of the earth. People who contact his business in Birmingham find themselves talking to employees, but never to the man himself. It's as though he's gone into hiding, and my guess is that he's very close to victory and doesn't want any distractions. If only I knew the answer."

He stopped as Henly appeared to clear away the soup plates and serve the next course. Meanwhile Dorina tried to think of a way to distract the Earl from this subject which was fraught with danger.

When they were alone again she said,

"So let us plan for the future of your horseless carriage. Have you decided on the next step?"

"There are one or two small technical problems to be overcome, but they won't take long. The steering needs a little attention."

"Tell me more."

She spoke only to distract his attention. She did not care about the steering, but she loved to hear him talk with such intensity.

And he did talk. All through the meal he discussed his work with a total confidence that Dorina could appreciate. In fact, she did not understand everything, but she knew she could follow more than any other woman would have been able to.

The Earl was good at explaining things, better than her beloved father had been, she had to admit. Many things became clear to her that had been obscure before. The whole wonderful world of engineering and inventions seemed to open out before her, as if for the first time.

At last the Earl said,

"Serve us coffee in the library, please Henly. Then everyone can go to bed."

When they were alone in the library he poured the coffee himself, while he talked on for another hour. It was about work, with nothing personal about it. Pistons, petrol, ignition, horse power – these were the words Dorina remembered afterwards.

But what she also remembered was the sense of vision, of standing on a high mountain and seeing as far as her inner eye could see. She wanted to stay there for ever.

At last he fell silent, watching her in the soft glow of the firelight.

"I've done all the talking and not let you say a word," he said.

"But I've enjoyed listening," she protested. "Now I know so much more than I did before. You make everything so easy to understand."

"Only to you," he said. "Now I must let you go to bed. I've kept you up so late that I shall not mind if you're a little late coming to work tomorrow morning."

“I shall be there at the usual time, my Lord,” Dorina said primly.

He laughed and held out a hand to help her to her feet.

They emerged into the hall to find just one light throwing a faint glow. Everyone else had gone to bed, and the house was quiet.

Dorina followed him up the main staircase. When they reached the first floor, her room was on the left while his was on the right. There were soft lights glowing where the passages turned.

“Goodnight,” Dorina said. “It was a wonderful evening. I have never enjoyed myself more.”

As she looked up at the Earl, she saw that he had a strange look in his eyes. It was quite different from the predatory admiration she had seen there at the Alhambra. Now there was sincerity and respect, as well as tenderness.

She caught her breath. It was almost too much for her.

“Goodnight, my Lord.”

“Goodnight – Dorina.”

In a daze she made her way to her room, resisting the temptation to look back and see if he was still watching her. When her door was safely closed she went to the mirror and surveyed herself.

She was still in the plain clothes she had worn all day, her hair pulled severely back. There seemed to be nothing alluring about the woman who faced her, nothing to tempt a man to draw closer.

And yet he had wanted to draw closer. Not because she was pretty but because their minds met. Their hearts too were meeting, although much must happen first. They were not ready, but it would happen soon.

She could dream about that.

*

Over the next few days, the Earl often took her to the factory to see the horseless carriage and show her how to drive it. Under his tutelage she became a very good driver, with an instinctive feel for what the vehicle could do.

"You've taken to this naturally," he told her, helping her down. "You might have been doing it all your life."

In a sense it was true she thought. She might not have been driving all her life, but she had been breathing in this atmosphere all her life. She should have told him long ago, but she had refused, wanting to enjoy this sweet time for a little longer.

But the time had come when she must be brave, whatever the consequences.

As they drove home she tried to think of the right words. When they reached the house she waited until they had gone inside before taking a deep breath and saying,

"My Lord, there's something I must tell you."

"One moment – " he had turned to the hall table where a letter lay, evidently having been delivered while they were out. He tore it open and an expression of delight spread over his face.

"Thank goodness!" he said, waving the contents. "I was afraid I might not be able to get them."

"Get what, my Lord?"

"Tickets. Theatre tickets. They're like gold dust. No, no – " he saw her expression and hastened to reassure her. "This isn't like that other time. These are for the Gaiety Theatre, where the greatest stars appear and royalty attends. I have a box. Do say you will share it with me."

"But when," she asked, half laughing at his boyish enthusiasm.

"Tonight. Say you'll come."

"Yes," she said, unable to resist him. "Of course I will."

"Be ready to leave in an hour."

She had a thrilling few minutes going through her clothes, overjoyed that once more she was free to dress up. Tonight she could look beautiful again, for him. All for him.

The dress she chose was gold satin and tulle. With it she wore a gold necklace and ear rings. She knew she looked fabulous and exotic, and a far cry from the business like female she had been recently. And when she descended the stairs, the Earl's eyes told her the same thing.

He too was dressed magnificently in white tie and tails. A glittering diamond adorned the frilly breast of his evening shirt, and for a moment she was swept back to the Alhambra and the man who had accosted her, fatuously sporting a fake diamond. But this time, instead of being upset, she could see the funny side.

"What is it?" he asked, seeing her smile.

"Nothing. A private joke." It would not be a good idea to remind him of the Alhambra.

"I wish you would not keep anything private from me."

"It isn't important."

"One day I will get to the heart of your mysteries. But I'll leave it for now."

It was a short journey to the Gaiety Theatre. They found a crowd outside, buzzing with excitement, as though awaiting some great event.

Looking at the posters, Dorina thought she knew what it was.

By Popular Acclaim the posters declared, *the return of the Great Actress – Lily Langtry. HER FIRST LONDON PERFORMANCE FOR MANY YEARS.*

"Lily Langtry," Dorina gasped. "Why, wasn't she – I mean – when I – that is – ?"

"She was the 'close friend and companion' of the Prince of Wales," the Earl supplied. "That's a very polite way of describing their relationship. I hope I haven't offended your sense of propriety."

"Yes – no – that is – "

Dorina answered vaguely because she was still shocked at herself for the slip she had almost just made. When she had said, "when I – ", she had meant to say, "when I met the Prince," and stopped herself just in time.

The Prince of Wales knew the value of a wealthy middle class, underpinned by successful entrepreneurs. It was even rumoured that when the horseless carriage was finally invented, he would be its first customer.

He had given several receptions for businessmen. John Radford had been invited to one and taken Dorina with him.

She could still remember the excitement of catching her first glimpse of the heir to the throne, and the extremely beautiful woman with him. Someone had whispered that it was Lily Langtry, the Prince's mistress.

All society knew that the middle-aged prince was a notorious womaniser, despite having a lovely wife and a large family.

Dorina had approached him with fascination, curtsied low, and been rewarded with five minutes of his attention, during which she had had the feeling that he was mentally stripping her clothes away. It was shocking, but she realised that he was a man of great charm.

Lily Langtry was also delightful. Dorina could see that the 'Jersey Lily', as she was known, really did have the perfect milk-maid complexion that her reputation claimed. She seemed unperturbed by her royal lover's wandering eye – possibly because she was so used to it.

Soon after that evening his eye had wandered away

from Lily altogether, and he had become devoted to the Countess of Warwick, his 'Darling Daisy'. Lily had gone to America to capitalise on her fame. Now she was back in London for a sell-out season.

They were almost the last to arrive, and the auditorium was already full to bursting point. The Earl led Dorina to a box in the first tier, and held the seat for her while she sat down.

"We're only just in time," he said. "The performance is about to begin."

That was lucky, she thought, realising that she was very conspicuous here. Although she had never moved in High Society, she had sometimes met those who did. Now she noticed several people down in the stalls whose faces she recognised and who might recognise her.

Thank heavens the theatre was lit by electricity, she thought. In a few moments the lights would go down and the darkness would shield her.

But before that could happen, the orchestra struck up loudly, and the audience rose to its feet applauding.

With horror, Dorina looked across at the box immediately opposite, and saw the Prince of Wales enter with Lady Warwick.

He stood there, handsome and smiling behind his dark red beard, just beginning to be tinged with grey. His air was genial. He knew that his future subjects loved him and forgave him his peccadilloes and he enjoyed this kind of occasion above all others.

Beside him, 'Daisy' Warwick stood, swathed in diamonds, supremely beautiful and assured.

Everyone acquainted with the Prince wanted to catch his eye. He nodded, giving the impression of responding to many at once, but the only one to whom he raised his hand, was the Earl.

'Heavens!' Dorina thought. 'He's looking straight across at us. Suppose he recognises me?"

She lowered her head, trying to reveal as little of her face as possible. To her relief the lights began to go down, and everyone could sit.

"Did you see who's with him?" the Earl murmured. "That's darling Daisy, of whom you may have heard."

"Who has not?" Dorina replied. "I suppose it's impossible for him to have a love affair without it being written about in the newspapers, and talked about incessantly."

"You are quite right," the Earl agreed. "That's one of the penalties of being a Prince, or even having an ordinary title, like myself. I am sure a good half-dozen people in the theatre tonight are wondering who is the lovely unknown lady by my side, and how far our love affair has gone."

Dorina laughed.

"Of course they are not thinking that," she replied. "They are merely thinking you are very smart, and they wish they were with you rather than the dull men they are sitting with."

The Earl laughed.

Then he said,

"You are here to feel romantic, and you certainly look romantic. So let us enjoy ourselves and not worry what anyone else may think of us."

"I wouldn't be so conceited as to expect them to think about me anyway," Dorina retorted.

"Then let me tell you that you are looking very lovely," the Earl said. "I think it would be difficult to find anyone to beat you."

Dorina smiled and teased him,

"I'm glad you said that before the curtain rose,

because you won't even notice me when Lily Langtry appears."

"You know what she looks like then?" he asked curiously.

"But of course. Everyone does, since her face has been used in so many advertisements," Dorina said, thinking quickly.

Then the curtain rose and she could breathe freely again.

The show was highly coloured and fast moving with wonderful tuneful music. Everything about it was brilliant.

First there was a chorus of elegantly dressed young ladies, dancing, turning this way and that, flirting over their shoulders at His Royal Highness.

The words of the song were a little risqué, but just within the bounds of propriety.

They were followed by a comedian with a vulgar manner and a very broad line of humour. Glancing across at the royal box, Dorina noticed that the Prince's sense of humour was evidently not subtle, as he roared with laughter at the broadest jokes.

Lady Warwick was different. She joined in the Prince's laughter, but only in a polite way. Obviously she was 'on-duty', keeping a jealous eye on her 'property'. Dorina wondered how she felt having to sit through a performance by the divine Lily.

At last, after a nicely-judged delay to whet the audience's appetite, there was a fanfare from the orchestra pit. On the stage a pair of glittering inner curtains parted to reveal the tall, voluptuous figure of a woman.

To loud applause she advanced to the front of the stage, moving gracefully, swinging her hips. Then she opened her arms, raising her head so that the whole theatre could see her dazzling smile.

Slowly she looked from left to right, taking in the whole theatre, and finally coming to the royal box. It might have been only imagination that her gaze lingered on the Prince.

The next moment she began to sing.

Too long away, too long apart,

What strange sensations in my heart.

The whole song was like that, a provocative ditty about good times past, lovers meeting again, sharing pleasure.

Remembering those things we shared,

Things spoken and unspoken,

Some that are secret for always.

But we both know those secrets,

We shall know them forever.

She finished with an outrageous wink at the royal box and the audience cheered. The Prince applauded, eyeing her with pleasure. Lady Warwick also applauded, but she was eyeing the Prince.

The Jersey Lily sang another song, even more suggestive than the first. When she had finished there was more applause, which she acknowledged graciously and with many smiles.

And it was clear that most of her smiles were for her royal admirer, who was waving to her, beaming.

"His Royal Highness is quite shameless," Dorina said.

"I'm afraid he is," the Earl agreed. "But can you blame him when women throw themselves at him all the time? And he's always interested in new conquests."

At that moment Dorina glanced across the theatre and saw that the Prince of Wales was looking in her direction, with a pair of binoculars.

She looked away quickly, hoping against hope that he had not seen her clearly, or remembered her from their last meeting. Thank goodness the performance was continuing.

But as the curtain fell for the interval the door to their box opened and a footman entered. Bowing to the Earl, he said,

"Lord Kennington?"

"Yes."

"His Royal Highness presents his compliments and hopes that you and your companion will join him in a small reception he is holding backstage during the interval."

"We shall be delighted," the Earl said. To Dorina he added, "You'll enjoy meeting the Prince."

"Oh no, I can't," Dorina said hurriedly. "I'm just a secretary. I'm not the sort of person who meets royalty."

"Is that what's troubling you? It's nonsense. You are entitled to meet anyone you want."

Now she understood. He was trying once more to make amends for the Alhambra, by showing her how high she stood in his esteem. At any other time she would have rejoiced, but tonight it was too dangerous.

"You are very kind, but you can't introduce your secretary," she said frantically. "He'll think you're mad."

"Not when he sees you. You mustn't worry if he flirts with you a little. He means no harm and I'll be there to look after you."

He rose and offered her his arm. Reluctantly Dorina took it and followed him out of the box. The footman led the way down a red-carpeted corridor.

Dorina knew that they were getting closer and closer to the moment when her pretence would be revealed. The Earl would know who she really was, and know too that she had deceived him. He would throw her out.

The reception room was crowded when they entered and there were several people in front of them, waiting to be presented to the Prince. This was her last chance to prevent a disaster. Only desperate measures would do.

She swayed, leaning dramatically against the Earl, who turned to her in alarm.

"Miss Martin! Good heavens, what is the matter?"

"I feel so faint," she whispered. "It's hot in here – *ooooooh!*"

The next moment she had 'fainted' dead away.

CHAPTER EIGHT

Dorina allowed herself to collapse against the Earl just as his arms went out to support her. She heard him call her name. The next moment he was lowering her to the floor, held against him.

"Miss Martin – Dorina!" he said hoarsely.

Through half open lids she could see his face leaning over hers, distraught.

"It's so hot in here," she gasped. "Take me out, quickly."

They were almost at the head of the line. The Earl looked around distractedly.

"Take me away," Dorina whispered. "I feel so ill."

A footman had seen what was happening and came towards them.

"Please give His Royal Highness my apologies," the Earl said. "As you can see, my companion is ill and I must leave with her."

"But you're nearly there," protested the footman. "Perhaps if you were to meet the Prince while the lady is cared for by others – "

Disaster! Dorina could not risk such a thing lest the Prince had recognised her, and mentioned her real name to the Earl.

She clung to him fiercely, saying, "Don't leave me. Please don't leave me."

"Never," he said fervently and rose with her in his arms.

He could see now that the Prince of Wales had observed him. Still holding Dorina's apparently fainting form, he managed to bow before hurrying away. The Prince inclined his head to signify that he understood his guest's predicament.

But when the Earl had gone he stared after him with a puzzled frown, until recalled to the present by a nudge from Lady Warwick.

Since his carriage was not due to arrive until the end of the performance, the Earl found a cab and laid Dorina gently inside. He got in beside her and the cab started to move. At once he tightened his arms, drawing her more closely to him.

"My dearest," he murmured. "My poor love. I'll soon have you home and safe."

She made a little contented sound and nestled against him. She was in heaven. She asked no more than this for the whole of her life.

"Dorina?" he said softly, making the word a question. "Dorina."

"Mmm?" she said happily.

"I just wanted to make sure I wasn't dreaming this. You feel so good in my arms."

"Yes, it feels good," she sighed.

The sound of her sigh did something to him. Unable to stop himself, he tipped her chin up with his fingers and kissed her urgently.

The feel of his lips on hers sent her into ecstasy, so that she sensed his urgency and responded with her own. Here in the darkness of the cab there was no need for false modesty. She could admit her passion in the movements of her hands and lips. She could kiss him and so reveal all her secrets that she could not tell him in words.

Her love swept over her making her feel shameless, wanton and blissfully happy. Soon he would say the words that her heart longed to hear.

At last he wrenched his lips from hers and spoke in a shaking voice.

"We're home."

"What?" she asked in a daze.

"We've arrived. Shall I help you out?"

"Thank you," she said shakily. Her whole body felt weak from what had just happened.

He helped her into the house, saying,

"Come into the library and I'll pour you a brandy."

Dorina agreed gladly. She did not want to end this perfect time with him. "I'm feeling much better now," she admitted.

Henly brought in the decanter and the Earl muttered something to him before he left.

"Here you are," he said, handing her a glass. "Drink it and it will make you feel better."

She sipped and felt a fiery sensation go through her.

"What a pity that you could not meet His Royal Highness," he said. "I'm sure you would have enjoyed it very much."

"Yes, it's such a pity."

"Never mind. I'll introduce you to him another time."

"That would be delightful," she said mechanically.

There was a silence. They both felt a little awkward with the memory of their passionate kisses. It had been dark and in the protective darkness they had been not only themselves but other people, free to express their passion.

But now they were in the light again and somehow their daytime selves got in the way.

"Why do you think you fainted?" he asked gently.

"Oh, it was only the heat," she replied.

"Strange. It didn't seem so very hot to me."

"Well – people react differently, don't they?"

"I would hate anything to happen to you."

Her heart turned over.

"I will be perfectly well after a good night's sleep."

"And that you will have as soon as you've seen the doctor."

"No, I don't need a doctor," Dorina said hastily.

There was a ring at the front door.

"That will be him now," said the Earl. I told Henly to send for him at once."

A moment later Henly announced,

"Dr. Jones, my Lord."

Dorina recognised the man who entered as the doctor who had attended the Earl on the night of the Alhambra.

He regarded her with interest, but she could see no sign of recognition.

"Miss Martin and I were at the Gaiety Theatre and she fainted just as we were about to meet the Prince of Wales," the Earl explained. "She says it was only the heat, but I would like to be sure it's nothing serious."

"My goodness," Dorina exclaimed with a laugh, "if every lady who fainted was presumed to be ill – "

"Ladies faint all the time and for trivial reasons," Dr. Jones agreed. "Sometimes a very lovely evening dress needs – shall we say? – severe restrictions?"

His eyes twinkled, and Dorina laughed back at his delicate way of mentioning stays.

"And sometimes the restrictions are overdone," she said.

"The point is, how do you feel now, madam."

"Perfectly well, thank you. There was really no need for his Lordship to call you at all."

"He was naturally very concerned for you. I'll give you a mild sleeping draught that will ensure you have a good night's rest. Dissolve this powder in water and in the morning you'll be completely well."

He bowed and let the Earl show him out. When they were safely in the hall, Dr. Jones allowed himself to speak freely, for they were old friends.

"You managed it then?"

"I beg your pardon?"

"The lady. I can see why she was worth the trouble. Did she manage to come and visit you in your sick-room in spite of the dragon?"

"The dragon?"

"Your secretary. I met her outside your room when I was here last and she scared the life out of me. Terrifying woman. Looked grim and sounded grim."

"But that – " The earl stopped and gave a faint smile.

"Goodnight," he said. "Thank you for coming out so late."

He was still smiling as he returned to the library.

"What is it?" Dorina asked.

"Did you meet the doctor when he was last here?"

"Yes, briefly, outside your door."

"What did you look like?"

"I had changed into my plainest clothes," she said with a touch of primness.

"I thought so. He didn't recognise you. He called my secretary 'the dragon'."

"And he didn't know it was me? Fancy that!"

"It's because you are two women," he continued. "You are my efficient companion and fellow engineer, who understands all my thoughts and actions. But you are also the most beautiful woman I have ever known. In fact I – "

He checked himself and added quickly,

"But I will say no more until you are quite recovered." He poured her a glass of cordial, saying as he gave it to her, "now take your powder and go to bed."

How she wished he had finished what he was going to say. But she knew the moment had passed. So she did as he said, slipping her arm through his as they walked up the stairs together.

He took her as far as her door, then gently disengaged himself.

"Goodnight, Dorina." His eyes were very tender.

"Goodnight, my Lord."

He watched until her door had closed behind her. Then he stood in silence for a long time, watching the door, almost as if he hoped it would open again.

At last he turned and went to his own room.

*

The sleeping draught soon took effect. When Dorina awoke next morning the sun was high in the sky and she knew that she had slept much longer than usual.

For some reason her dreams, and now her thoughts, were full of her parents and the love they had shared.

She had often wondered why her father had not

remarried. Then he would have been less lonely and he might have had a son.

But from some of the things he had said to her, she realised that, because he had been so devoted to her mother and her mother to him, he would have thought it wrong or perhaps degrading to put anyone else in her place.

"Your mother was everything I thought of, dreamt of and wanted, since I was old enough to think women attractive," he had once told her. "The very first time I saw her, I fell in love and knew she was what I had been looking for all my life."

"I'm sure she felt the same about you," Dorina had said.

"It was love at first sight for both of us," he had replied. "We were blissfully happy, even though there were difficulties and troubles to be overcome."

He had looked thoughtful before he continued,

"I was busy trying to make my business the largest and the most important of its kind in England."

Dorina knew this was true and he was not boasting.

At the same time she thought how lonely he must often have felt when her mother was dead and he came home at night to an empty house.

'I should have been jealous,' she thought, 'if he'd had a son whom he loved more than me. At the same time the weight must have crushed him, and eventually became too much for him.'

If there had been a soft loving wife to come home to, then perhaps he would not have worked as he often did, all through the night and gobbled down skimpy meals.

'He would have done it for her, but for nobody else," she thought.

That was love.

The love which so far she had not encountered.

Men had paid her compliments.

Men had tried to kiss her but, because she was always on the move, no sooner had she made friends with a family in Italy, her father would ask her to move on to some other country whose language she had not yet learnt.

She wanted to weep

She wanted to reach out and put back the years and stay with him rather than go abroad.

But now it was too late.

'At least they are together,' she thought. 'And that is the only way they could be truly happy.'

She wondered why, just at this moment, she was haunted by thoughts of the love that her parents had shared.

Then she saw the Earl's face in her mind, his delightful smile. She heard the gentle note in his voice that he seemed to keep just for her.

And she knew why her mind and her heart were filled with thoughts of love.

It seemed to her now that the world was a different place. Nothing was the same since the Earl's kiss.

She felt as if his lips were still touching hers and that strange feeling was still moving in her heart.

"This is love," she told herself. "I have fallen in love with him. It wasn't a wise thing to do, but that no longer matters. It is done."

She lay thinking of the wonder of the Earl's kiss and how much it had meant to her even though she could not put it into words.

'If this is love,' she thought, 'it is even more wonderful than I expected it to be.'

Then almost as if someone was pulling her down from the heights of happiness, she remembered that the Earl had not said anything final.

He had kissed her, and paid her compliments, but he had said nothing that committed him to her as she felt committed to him.

And yet, surely, he had come to the verge of declaring his love last night.

'Perhaps it's as well,' she thought. 'First I must go to Birmingham, and sort matters out there. Then I can return and tell him everything about myself. Or can I return?'

In Birmingham everything would change. The people who worked for her father would be aware for the first time that he was no longer with them, and that she had taken his place.

It would mean leaving her work here, leaving the Earl, perhaps for ever. For when he knew the truth, perhaps he would no longer care for her.

But in truth, how much did he really care? He was a man who had always taken love lightly.

'Easy come, easy go' she thought. 'Perhaps, for all his words about understanding his mind, I am just a passing fancy to him.'

She made a sudden decision. She would tell him everything today. The thought lightened her heart.

Her maid entered with her breakfast.

"It's a lovely day, miss," she said chattily. "The master told us to let you sleep late."

"That was kind of him. What time is it?"

"Past ten o'clock, miss."

"Goodness! I must eat quickly and get to work. How is his Lordship this morning?"

"He's gone away, miss. He asked me to give you this when you woke."

She handed Dorina a sealed letter, and went away.

Hurriedly she opened the letter, and read,

My dear Dorina,

How sorry I am to leave before you woke, but I have just received a message from my mother, asking me to visit her. She is having some problems with my young sister Celia, and wants me to play the heavy-handed older brother.

I don't believe that anything is truly amiss. Celia is a delightful girl, although a little wilful. But I suppose I must attend and set Mama's mind at rest. It will also give me the chance to discuss another matter of importance with her.

I will probably be away for a week. I command you to rest and do as little as possible until I return.

Gerald.

Dorina's first thought, on reading this, was dismay. He had vanished and left her alone just when she longed to see him.

But then she saw that she had been given a wonderful chance. Now she had the time to visit Birmingham, set things in order and return to London before the Earl did.

Everything seemed to be working to help her.

Before she had even finished breakfast, Mr. Johnson arrived to see her.

"I had some things to see to in London," he said, "and I called to urge you to come to Birmingham as soon as possible."

"Then I will come today," she replied eagerly.

She spoke to Henly, telling him that she too, like the Earl, had been unexpectedly called home, but would return soon.

"But where shall I tell his Lordship you are?" Henly asked, worried. "He will want your address."

"There is no need," she assured him. "I will be back before he is."

A cab arrived to take them to the station. In a short time her luggage was loaded onto it and the two of them were on their way.

Dorina could not help looking out of the window as the house disappeared. If things went badly, she knew she might be saying goodbye to everything that had made her happy.

When they were settled into the train and it had started its journey, Mr. Johnson said,

"I thought that, before you speak to your father's people and tell them that you have taken his place, you would want to see where he is buried."

"Where have you put him?" Dorina asked.

"The doctors told me that it was impossible for them to go on hiding him. The only thing was for him to be buried, without anyone knowing."

"And you managed to do that?"

"He was buried next to your mother at midnight. And no one in the village had the slightest idea what was happening.

"Those who had nursed him were told that they must keep his death a secret until the newspapers were informed and they kept their word."

There was silence for a moment. Then Dorina said,

"I'm glad you buried him next to my mother. It's where he would want to be. Did anyone pray over him?"

"I found a vicar who lives at the other end of the county. He had never met your father and knew nothing about him."

"Was he curious?" Dorina asked.

"Not particularly. The doctors told him it was a man with few relations, whose death had to be kept quiet until they were informed. We told him they were far away, visiting another country."

"You've been very kind and very helpful," Dorina said.

"Tell me, have you used your time to good advantage?" he asked. "Have you learned anything with the Earl?"

Dorina gave a deep sigh.

"Oh yes," she said. "Many things."

It was true that she had learned many things, some of them had been about his work, but she had learned much about herself and her own heart.

'I love him, I love him,' she thought as they drove on. 'But what can the future hold for us? When he learns the truth he will think the worst of me and everything will be over between us. How naïve I was to think that it could be otherwise.'

It was late in the afternoon before they reached her home. It was a grand old house, beautiful and luxurious, but very lonely.

She had a sudden feeling that it was almost too much to see it again, to know it was empty of everyone she loved.

'I may have to live here alone, completely alone,' she told herself and wanted to cry.

"Stay and dine with me tonight," she asked Mr. Johnson. "I'll return soon."

"Thank you. While you're gone I'll write some letters."

She took the carriage and drove to the little church. There she found the family vault and knelt before it, weeping.

'Help me,' she prayed. 'I don't know what to do.'

She was not sure whether she was praying to God, or to her parents in Heaven. But when she rose she felt that, wherever they were at this moment, her father and mother were thinking of her and loving her.

It was late when she left the church and went back to the great house that was now hers.

Mr. Johnson had just finished his letters, and despatched a footman to post them urgently.

As they sat down to dinner he said,

"You have not yet told me what you learnt from Lord Kennington?"

Dorina drew in her breath.

'If I told him the truth,' she thought, 'he would certainly be surprised. But I cannot tell him everything.'

"Really very little," she said. "He had so many letters, which had nothing to do with business."

"Did you manage to discover if he really is advanced with his horseless carriage?"

"It's very hard to say," she replied cautiously, "since I do not really understand what you would consider advanced. And, of course, I have no way of comparing his invention with our own design."

"You'll see ours tomorrow," he assured her. "And you'll meet a lot of your workforce. Then, the day after, I'm hoping to put the horseless carriage on display.

"Those letters I've just sent were to potential customers. They should arrive first post tomorrow, and I think people will abandon any other plans and hurry here to see the sensation of the age."

"The sensation of the age," Dorina murmured, thinking of the beautiful carriage that the Earl had shown her.

"I think we'll get ahead of our rivals," said Mr. Johnson with glee. "I'm sure Lord Kennington has not yet shown his carriage to customers."

"That would certainly put us in an advantageous

position," Dorina said carefully.

She was caught in a trap. In the next few days she would be challenging the man she loved and in a way that could destroy his dreams.

And there was nothing she could do to prevent it. If she held back on her own carriage, she would be betraying the faithful men who had worked so hard for her father and whose work had brought success so close.

When Mr. Johnson had left, Dorina went up to her room and found it cold and empty.

"Oh, but you're not in here any more, miss," said the housekeeper. "You're in the master's old room."

So she knew that he was dead. Of course, all the servants must know. But they had said nothing and loyally kept the secret.

The housekeeper formally escorted Dorina to her father's old room, which she found freshly cleaned with a fire in the grate as the evening was chilly.

"Thank you, Hannah," she said. "This was very thoughtful of you."

"It was only right and proper, miss," Hannah said. "This is the master's room. And you're the master now."

'Master' Dorina noted. Not 'mistress'.

And that was right, for it was a man's work she had to do here. In their own way her servants had let her know what they expected of her. Tomorrow her work force would let her know the same.

And this was their right for they depended on her. Her own feelings did not matter.

The trap was closing on her.

CHAPTER NINE

Dorina dressed with great care the next day. She was in mourning for her father and now for the first time, she could acknowledge this. So she chose a black dress. Her hat and gloves were black. Anyone seeing her would understand the truth at once.

Mr. Johnson had evidently had the same idea, for he too was dressed in black when he arrived at the house to collect her.

"I've ordered your entire Birmingham workforce to congregate in the Hatton factory," he said. "Are you ready?"

"Ready for anything," she replied.

They drove to the Hatton factory, which was the largest of the three Birmingham establishments. The place was already buzzing with life when they arrived.

Both men and women were arriving, for John Radford had employed many females in the offices of his factories.

They turned their heads at the sound of the carriage arriving, and smiled at the sight of Dorina. But their smiles faded when they saw how she was dressed.

At last she stood before them on a platform in the main workshop. Now a hush had fallen, as they had begun to suspect what they were about to hear.

Mr. Johnson spoke first. In grave tones he confirmed that John Radford had died and had been buried quietly.

"The secrecy was necessary in order not to alert our rivals. They might think that his demise heralded a period of weakness in this company. If so, they were mistaken. We may no longer have John Radford, but we have his heir and his chosen successor, Miss Dorina Radford."

There was a moment of shock, for it was unheard of to have a woman taking charge of a commercial enterprise. But most of the people here knew her, at least by sight, and she was a link to the man they had admired. So, after that first quiet moment, they burst into applause.

Mr. Johnson stood back and indicated to Dorina to come forward. The applause increased, but at last there was silence.

This was it, the moment she had known must come, when she must assume her inheritance and her responsibilities, whatever the cost.

She spoke movingly of her father and the great industrial empire he had created. Then she turned their thoughts to the future.

"My father would have wanted us to carry on in the pioneering spirit with which he inspired us," she cried. "I shall do my part, but it rests with you, whether we gradually die away, or go forward and bring great new inventions to our country like the horseless carriage, which is going to lead a revolution. I believe that we will be at the head of that revolution – where we ought to be."

One or two people began to clap but Dorina raised her hand and went on,

"We will increase our production year by year with new ideas and new inventions. You have been marvellous so far in keeping us ahead in engineering in this country. I can only beg of you to go on getting better and better every year, as you have done in the past."

She sat down amidst tumultuous applause.

It was done. The die was cast. Now all the world would know that John Radford was dead and the torch had passed to his daughter. From this moment there was no going back.

There were more speeches as the senior members of staff welcomed her and pledged their loyalty. Then with enormous pride, they led her to the place where the horseless carriage stood waiting.

Dorina braced herself, but it was still a shock to see a machine that looked so similar to the one she had seen in the Earl's workshop. With every eye on her, she tried to remember that she was supposed to be seeing such an invention for the first time.

They showed her how it worked, and she exclaimed with wonder, while all the time she was noticing how exactly alike it was to the Earl's. The differences were tiny.

She was introduced to the company driver, a man called Jeremiah Conway. He got behind the wheel and began to drive the machine around. There was applause and, to everyone's satisfaction, Miss Radford applauded harder than anyone.

Mr. Conway leaned down to her.

"Would you like to sit beside me?" he asked, reaching out a hand to her.

She took it, climbing into the passenger seat, and suddenly she was back in an earlier time, when she and the Earl had sat side by side behind the wheel of his carriage.

She sat there while the carriage went around again and then she said,

"I would like to drive."

There were murmurs of approval. Everyone admired her spirit and were astonished when she managed to drive all around the workshop without mishap. But nobody suspected that she had done this before.

She could not help observing that the steering was not quite as smooth as that on the Earl's vehicle. But there was nothing she could say.

'How can I bear this?' she asked herself. 'I deceived him and now I'm deceiving them. But I never meant to deceive anybody.'

At last the occasion was over. Dorina left to the accompaniment of cheers, and went home to prepare for the great dinner Mr. Johnson had organised for that night at Birmingham's most prestigious hotel.

For that dinner she wore black again, but this time it was a black evening gown, adorned with diamonds. She looked stately and magnificent and conveyed an impression of prosperity, which she knew was what her workers needed to see.

At eight o'clock she made her entrance into the Grand Hotel, sweeping into the great banqueting hall on Mr. Johnson's arm. Eighty of her senior staff rose to greet her with more applause.

This time it had a slightly different sound. Earlier that day they had been unsure of her. Now they had transferred their trust to her. They accepted her.

There were more speeches, but this time they came from the senior workers, welcoming their new employer and promising her their loyalty.

Then the speeches altered slightly in tone and became a hymn of praise to the horseless carriage and what it would mean for the future of the world.

"Others have sought to get ahead of us," one speaker said. "The Earl of Kennington is our greatest rival, but he has not achieved what we have achieved. Our technology is superior to anything he has."

Dorina kept the smile on her face, but inwardly she knew that this was not so.

'He will hear of this dinner,' she thought. 'He will know I sat here and heard him abused.'

She was in agony, but she was still trapped.

At last the evening was over. As he saw her to her carriage, Mr. Johnson said,

"Sleep well tonight. We have a very big day ahead of us tomorrow. In fact – "

He broke off. Dorina frowned, wondering at a suppressed excitement in his manner.

"What is it?" she asked. "What were you going to say?"

"Nothing, nothing. Just something I planned – well, I'm hoping for – it's very unlikely but miracles do happen."

"Won't you tell me what it is?"

"No, that would be unlucky. Let's just wait and see. Goodnight."

He stepped back quickly, signalling her driver to start, so that she was unable to ask him any more.

All the way home Dorina was puzzling about his strange words and even stranger manner.

'He's normally such a businesslike man,' she thought. 'Suddenly he seems to have taken off on a flight of fancy. I wonder what he's keeping up his sleeve.'

The exhilaration of the day stayed with her until she had gone to bed. But then, in the darkness and silence, she remembered the Earl and the feel of his kisses came back to her.

'How is it possible,' she asked herself, 'that a kiss could be so wonderful that, in some strange way, I can still feel in my heart what I felt at that moment?

'Where is he now? What is he doing? Is he thinking of me?'

As she shut her eyes and tried to go to sleep, she felt

that her heart was breaking.

'There is no way back for me now,' she thought. 'I should have stayed in London. I love him, I love him. If he wanted me, I would still be prepared to go on being his secretary.'

But then she knew that was not true.

She had to keep faith with the people who relied on her.

She wanted to show her father, if he was watching, that she could be as good as any son he might have had.

'That is my duty in the future,' she thought. 'If I am lonely then I can merely cry at night as I am crying now, because I have known love and lost it.'

On that thought she fell asleep.

*

Next morning she dressed in clothes that were severe but fashionable. All the way to the factory she was remembering Mr. Johnson's strange excitement, and wondering what it meant.

The great workshop was festive. Down one wall were long tables set with food and wine.

In the centre of the floor stood the horseless carriage, surrounded by a rope barrier. Four men, one at each corner, were on guard to prevent spectators from coming too close.

"Are we ready to start?" she asked Mr. Johnson.

"Not quite," he said. "There'll need to be a small delay while we wait for the guest of honour."

If anything, Mr. Johnson's excitement was even more pronounced than ever.

"But who is the guest of honour? You never mentioned him before."

"That is because I wasn't sure he would come. Even

now I won't believe it until I see him coming through that door, although I was sent a most encouraging message – "

"Mr. Johnson," Dorina said patiently. "Who are you talking about?"

"Why, the Prince of Wales, of course," he said in a hushed voice.

"You cannot mean that."

"But of course. It is well known that the Prince is avid to own the first horseless carriage. And when he buys one, the whole of society will follow."

"But he surely cannot mean to come here?"

"He is currently paying a visit to the Marquis of Glandon, who lives only five miles from here. I sent a message to Glandon Towers, inviting the Prince to a special presentation.

"I knew there was only a faint chance that he would accept such a late invitation, but it was a risk worth taking. And I've had a message in return to say that he will come 'if possible'."

Dorina stared.

"Are you serious?"

"Absolutely, I swear it. I didn't say anything before because I didn't think it would happen. He still might not arrive, but suppose he did – "

"Mr. Johnson you are a genius," Dorina said, awed. "If the Prince buys one of our vehicles we will lead the revolution."

She stopped as a thought came to her.

"And if he doesn't buy one, we'll *give* him one. As long as we can tell people that he possesses a *Radford* horseless carriage, that's all that necessary. The newspapers will talk about it and we'll be established as the leaders in this field."

It was Mr. Johnson's turn to be awed.

"That is brilliant," he said. "I can see you have a natural talent for this business, Miss Radford."

"And even if the Prince doesn't come, we can still make him the gift," she mused. "Of course, it would be better if he did come. Do we have any newspapers here, by the way?"

"Oh yes, several. In some cases the editor himself has insisted on being present. This is a big moment, and nobody wants to miss it."

"But they don't know about the Prince?"

"Oh no. I've kept that possibility a secret, because if he doesn't arrive we would look foolish."

"But how can we begin? Protocol dictates that nothing starts until royalty has arrived, but if we don't know when, or if, he's coming – "

"I think things are already happening, whether we're ready or not," Mr Johnson said, eyeing the throng that was growing every moment. "The customers, the reporters, they're all hanging around the carriage, each one trying to sneak a better look than his neighbours."

"Then we must go and talk to them, and His Royal Highness must take his chances," Dorina said firmly.

Things could not be going better, but there was a little ache in her heart that she knew she must suppress.

With her head high, Dorina made a stately entrance, knowing that all eyes were upon her. Today was the day she would honour dear Papa, and make him proud of her.

She spoke little, leaving most of the talking to the designers and engineers who knew all the technical details. She understood that her presence was partly symbolic. She was the sign that Radford's would go on and she made a good talking point for the reporters.

A group of them converged on her, begging for some kind of statement. She replied by stressing her father's achievements and how proud he would be on this day.

Suddenly a buzz went round the crowd. There was a commotion at the entrance, the great double doors were pulled back wide enough to allow a coach and horses to be driven through.

"He's here," Mr. Johnson hissed in her ear.

The next moment a cheer went up as everyone in the crowd recognised the Prince of Wales.

He descended from the carriage, followed by his host, the Marquis of Glandon, and various other followers.

In a daze, Dorina came forward and curtsied. The Prince drew her to her feet and smiled directly into her eyes.

"Miss Radford, what a pleasure to meet you again. I had heard you were abroad, but I had a strange feeling that you had returned quite recently."

Then he winked.

If Dorina had any doubts that he had recognised her at the theatre, they were dispelled by his next words, uttered in a low voice.

"We must have a little talk before I leave. I'm alive with curiosity."

"As Your Royal Highness pleases," she murmured.

Then to the breathless delight of the spectators, the Prince became absorbed in the carriage and demanded to be driven on a short trip.

He was assisted into the passenger seat and everyone stood back while the engine was cranked up. Then the carriage moved slowly round the shed and out into the yard. The Prince smiled broadly all the time.

"Not a hitch!" said Mr. Johnson, by Dorina's side. "It's moving perfectly. We've done it. Oh, I wish I could see

Kennington's face when he realises we've outsmarted him."

"You can," said a voice behind them.

An icy hand seemed to clutch Dorina's heart. Oh, surely it could not be true. It could not be –

Frozen with horror, she turned and found herself looking at the Earl, who stood there, his eyes filled with bitterness and fury.

Her heart almost stopped and for a moment she was unable to speak. He saw this, and his lip curled with contempt.

"Good day to you, *Miss Radford,"* he said. "I trust matters are going well for you."

"I – very well, thank you," she stammered.

"I can't tell you how *unexpected* it is to find you here. But perhaps it should not have been unexpected. Maybe a sensible man would have guessed the truth long ago."

"Please – if you'll only let me explain – "

"But my dear Miss Radford, no explanation is necessary. Now I know your true identity, I see that everything that happened was inevitable. One who carries such responsibilities as yours can be forgiven if she forgets a few other things – like truth, honour and fair dealing."

Incensed at hearing his employer spoken to thus, Mr. Johnson took a step forward and said hotly,

"Sir, I don't know who you are but – "

"Then I am sure Miss Radford will be only too happy to tell you," the Earl said with a cold smile.

"This is the Earl of Kennington," Dorina told Mr Johnson.

His eyes widened in outrage.

"In that case, my Lord, allow me to say that you should not be here. With all due respect you are our rival and there are secrets here that – that – "

"Calm yourself," the Earl told him. "If I looked closely at your horseless carriage, I doubt if I would find many things I had not seen before. Is that not so, Miss Radford?"

"Whatever does he mean?" Mr. Johnson asked her.

"He means," replied Dorina stormily, "to be insulting. You need not think I don't understand you, sir."

"I was sure you would for I know you are very clever. Of course, just how clever is something I didn't appreciate until now. My compliments, madam. You have achieved a considerable trick. You took me in totally, and that was something I had not believed possible. Good day to you."

He inclined his head and turned away. Dorina stared after him, feeling furious and wretched at the same moment.

On the one hand she felt she could not blame him for what he was thinking. But on the other hand, she had a temper and it was rising now. How *dare* he think such things of her, however it looked?

Eyes glittering with anger, she turned and laid her hand on Mr. Johnson's arm and walked away with him.

After that she said and did all the right things, but she was functioning like a robot, for her mind was elsewhere. Vaguely she was conscious that the day was a triumph, but what did that matter beside the fury and betrayal she had seen in the Earl's eyes?

At last the Prince took her aside, as he had promised. With a chuckle in his voice, he said,

"That wasn't a real faint, was it? My guess is that Kennington didn't know who you were, and you were afraid I would give you away. Well, I probably would have done, so you were rather clever."

"Thank you, Your Royal Highness."

"What little game were you playing? Studying his secrets, I suppose. So, what's yours in that carriage, and what's his?"

"Sir, I was not spying on him. I merely went to work for him to learn about business. And then," Dorina added forlornly, "everything went wrong."

"He fell in love with you. Surely that's something that went right?"

"He's not in love with me, sir."

The Prince chuckled.

"I know better. He couldn't take his eyes off you when he should have been looking at the stage. I know that because I was watching your box myself. Mostly I looked at you, but whenever I looked at him, *he* was looking at *you*."

Despite everything her heart leapt with instant happiness. Then she remembered what was happening, and knew she would never be happy again.

"It is no use, sir," she said. "He thinks the worst of me, and now he always will. I didn't spy on him, but he won't believe me. Everything is over between us."

The Prince of Wales considered.

"Maybe not," he said. "Who knows what may happen? *Why, look who's here!"*

Startled at his sudden exclamation, Dorina looked up to find the Earl standing before them. His face was hard as he surveyed her in conversation with the Prince.

"Kennington, my dear fellow," the Prince exclaimed jovially, seizing the Earl by the hand and pumping it up and down, apparently oblivious to the freezing atmosphere.

"I must admit, I didn't expect to see you here," His Royal Highness continued. "Into the lions' den, so to speak. Did you have to fight your way past the guards?"

"No, I just walked in quietly," the Earl said. "I had not known that you would be here, sir, but since you are, may I take the opportunity to advise you against making a hasty decision?"

"Ah, you want to sell me your own vehicle. But is it ready, my dear chap?"

"Yes, sir, it is. I was preparing to have just such a day as this and to invite you to it. I venture to say that my horseless carriage can do anything that the Radford model can achieve. I believe it to be faster, stronger and far more reliable."

"And you want me to see it before I commit myself, eh? Well, that sounds very fair."

"Thank you, sir. When you return to London – "

"Oh my dear fellow, I'm far too impatient for that. I want it here by tomorrow. Send a telegram to your works and have them transport it by rail.

"You'll need to hire an engine. It might be best if I give the order for that. It'll make them more co-operative. And I'm sure you've got some sort of wagon that they can hitch onto the back of the engine.

"When it reaches the station you can hitch horses to the wagon to take it the last lap."

"You mean, bring my vehicle to the Radford workshops?" the Earl asked, rebellion in his eyes.

"No, of course not. Bring it to Glandon Towers. Ah, Glandon old friend, there you are. Come and hear the plans I'm making to turn your estate upside down."

The Marquis of Glandon had been hovering in the background for the last few moments. Now he came forward, smiling with pleasure.

"My estate is at your disposal, sir."

"Then here's my idea. We'll have a race in your grounds tomorrow. Miss Radford will bring her vehicle, and Kennington will bring his. They'll compete, side by side, and we'll see which one is the victor."

CHAPTER TEN

She was back in Grosvenor Square, opening the mail, then ready to take it to the man she loved – the man she had loved from the first, she now realised.

Through the mist of her dreams she saw herself, almost dancing towards his room, filled with joy because she was going to see him again.

When she had entered his room he had smiled at her, saying,

"Good morning. What have you brought me today? Is it good or bad?"

"That depends on you," Dorina had often replied. "Some of them sound good, but there's always the question of whether you'll be bored."

"If it's another dance or dinner party given for idiotic young debutantes who giggle when I talk to them and blush when I pay them a compliment, then I certainly will be," the Earl had answered.

"But I'm sure they are delighted with your compliments."

"Of course they are. All women want compliments, and if you don't give them willingly they are dragged out of you. Did you notice their new hat, do you think they dance better than anyone else you've danced with?"

He spoke scathingly and Dorina had laughed.

"Now you're asking too much," she had said. "Women do their best but men have always had their own way."

"That's what you think. I assure you we men are deceived, lied to and eventually defrauded, simply because we've been foolish enough to be captured by a pretty face. What man has not been entranced by beauty and a soft voice which paid him compliments he didn't deserve?"

"Well, if he didn't deserve the compliments he should have known better than to be captured," she had teased him, laughing. "It's entirely his own fault."

"You are very hard on us poor men."

"Poor men, nonsense! Look what advantages a man has. Strength, good looks and in many cases a title."

"Are you saying you think that's enough?" he demanded.

"More than enough."

"I'd have appreciated it if you'd added, 'a brilliant brain like yours, sir.'"

"Now you are asking for compliments. You know if I paid them to you, you'd suspect me of asking for a larger salary or saying that I feel unappreciated."

"You always manage to get the last word," he said with a grin. "As I've pointed out many times, I couldn't do without you."

Afterwards Dorina had often remembered him saying that and wished it were true.

Now as the clouds parted, bringing her to wakefulness she remembered it again.

She sat up in her bed, realising that the pretty dream was over. She was no longer in Grosvenor Square, exchanging teasing ripostes with him, full of hope for the future. She was back in Birmingham, in her real world where she had come to take command and where she had forfeited the Earl's love.

'How could I have been so naïve as to imagine I could just come here for a few days and then return to London as though nothing had happened?' she mused. 'Now there's no turning back, and all is over between us. He hates me. Perhaps he's right to hate me. And he will never, never kiss me again.'

She was seized with passionate longing for that forbidden kiss. But it was as far away as the moon and the stars, and she felt the tears trickling down her cheeks as some of his words came back to her, ominously.

'We men are deceived, lied to and eventually defrauded, simply because we've been foolish enough to be captured by a pretty face.'

He had spoken in fun, but how ominously true they must seem to him now.

If only she could talk to him and explain, but would she have the chance to get near him today? Did he really care enough to listen now that he had triumph within his grasp.

Just the fact that the race was happening was a kind of success. Whatever had been the Prince's intention when he intervened yesterday, it had made everything worse for Dorina and Radford's.

Most of her potential gains had been lost in a moment. The customers who had been on the verge of placing orders had held back, meaning to watch the race, and decide which one to buy according to the result.

The Marquis of Glandon had thrown open his grounds so that everyone who wanted to could come and watch the race. Some would come for the vehicles, some would come to see the Prince of Wales, but whatever the reason, the crowds would be large. Whichever of the two horseless carriages won, the world would be there to witness the victory.

'I cannot complain,' she sighed to herself. 'Radford Engineering tried to get ahead of the Earl and he has turned the tables on us.'

After the Prince's dramatic gesture the previous day, everyone had been full of excitement. People had rushed hither and thither, sending telegrams, making arrangements.

Gradually the crowd broke up. Everybody now had urgent things to do.

At Radford's they were busy creating transport for the carriage. It was designed and built in little more than two hours, and looked like a large raft on wheels. Four horses were harnessed, ready for the slow careful journey to Glandon Towers that would be made the following morning.

But the big journey was the one taken by the Earl's vehicle from London.

The engine, drawing the huge wagon, with the horseless carriage strapped on top, had travelled on past Birmingham Station to Glandon Halt, a tiny station on a branch line that had been put there for the convenience of the Glandon family. From there it was only a short distance to the estate.

By chance one of Dorina's servants happened to see it arrive, since he had gone there to collect some goods from another train.

"You never saw such a commotion in your life, ma'am," he told Dorina when he had returned home. "Lord Kennington was there, giving everyone orders, terrified in case the machine was damaged. And there was such a to-do, uncoupling it from the train and getting it onto the road, then attaching the horses."

"Where did they take it?" Dorina asked.

"I spoke to one of the men from Glandon Towers,

ma'am, and he said it was going to the estate. Lord Kennington is staying there tonight."

'So he would dine with the Prince,' Dorina thought, 'and would have ample opportunity to talk to him and persuade him of the merits of his own carriage.'

She herself would not see him until ten o'clock next morning, which was when her party was scheduled to arrive.

But far more important than seeing the Prince was the fact that she would see the Earl. Would she have a chance to talk to him alone? Could she make him understand?

Now the fateful morning had arrived and as she travelled to the factory to meet up with Mr. Johnson and the others, her heart warned her that she was about to lose everything.

They arrived at Glandon Towers at exactly ten o'clock and found the great gates already open. Lord Glandon met them and took them to the start of the road on which they would race.

"We're going to travel round it first in my carriage," he said, "so that everyone can become familiar with it beforehand. Then we'll all go into the house for lunch and by that time His Royal Highness might be awake."

The journey round the estate was an ordeal. Dorina sat in the carriage with the Earl and he took no notice of her at all. His face was hard and set against her. Her temper rose.

When the journey ended they went into the great house and a butler showed them the way to the drawing room, where coffee and cakes awaited.

But as they were walking towards the drawing room, Dorina seized the Earl's arm.

"I would like to talk to you," she said.

He looked surprised.

"I see no need."

"But I do. I will not have you ignoring me."

"I suggest it's better if you also ignore me."

Dorina gritted her teeth, refusing to back down.

"Don't force me to make a scene in public, my Lord."

He saw the determination in her face and yielded with a slight shrug, letting her draw him into the nearest room.

As soon as she had shut the door behind her, Dorina said in an imploring voice,

"I know you must think I betrayed you, but I truly never meant to."

"My dear lady, I am sure you've convinced yourself, but when I recall that you came under a false name and carefully concealed the fact that you were my rival's daughter and about to take over his firm – well, I think betrayal is the right word."

He had never before spoken to her in such a harsh voice and she flinched. For a moment she was on the verge of tears, but she fought them back. She would not be a weeping, wailing female. She would face up to her mistakes.

"That was wrong of me," she said, "but it was innocently done. It's true that I have to take over the firm and I realised how little I knew. I came to you to learn about business – "

"No, you came to learn about *my* business," he interrupted her coldly. "To spy on me."

"You are wrong my Lord," she said proudly. "Radford's leads in every aspect of engineering and it would never occur to me to spy on your creations. Why should I when ours are better?"

"Come," he retorted, "you're not pretending that your horseless carriage is better than mine, are you? Although I can well believe that it's vastly improved since you've seen mine."

"If you're suggesting that I passed on any of your ideas to my engineers, you are very mistaken," she said hotly. "I was careful never to do so."

"To be sure!"

"I am telling the truth."

"Give me one reason why I should believe you."

She took a deep breath.

"Because I love you."

"No!" The word was a shout of horror. "No more of that. When I think of the things I said to you – the feelings I expressed – " He put his hands to his head and strode about the room.

At last he rounded on her, his face distraught.

"Let me tell you something that will complete your satisfaction at what you've done to me. I went to see my mother and I told her about you, how much I loved you, how I had met the one woman in the world I could want to marry.

"And my mother told me to come home and fetch you and take you back with me, so that she can meet you. She was delighted that I had found a woman I wanted to marry and was ready to give us her blessing.

"So I came hurrying back, full of joy at the thought of seeing you again, of telling you the news and taking you to meet my mother. I pictured how we would spend the journey planning our wedding – "

He stopped. Dorina regarded him with horror. She could sense his pain across the distance he was keeping between them, something almost tangible.

"I'm sorry," she whispered.

"Wait, I haven't finished. The story gets even better. I arrived home to find you vanished. Not a word of warning, not a letter, and no address to tell me where you'd gone. I nearly went out of my mind.

"I couldn't bear being in the house, so I went to the factory, where I was accosted by one of my workers who had recently joined us.

"He'd seen you when I took you there and told me that you reminded him of someone, but he couldn't remember who. Suddenly it had come to him. He'd once worked at Radford's you see and he'd seen you there. It was a few years ago, which was why he didn't recognise you at once. But now he was certain that this woman was Dorina Radford."

"Oh no, no."

He gave a harsh laugh.

"I said the same. No! I didn't believe it. It was impossible that the woman I trusted above all others had deceived me, entrancing me with her beauty, while all the while spying on me.

"I tried so hard not to believe him, but as long as I didn't know where you were, the doubt was there. So I took the next train to Birmingham and discovered the result of all your treachery and scheming. The Prince of Wales, all ready to buy your product and ignore mine."

"He wasn't ignoring yours. You've kept it shrouded in secrecy."

"Except to you," he shouted.

It took him a moment to recover himself after that outburst. Then he went on,

"Luckily I was able to intervene and get him to wait, to test one vehicle against another. When he sees them side by side, it won't matter how many ideas you've stolen from me."

"I swear I didn't – "

"Be silent. Do you think I want to hear you speak? For what? More lies? More deceptions? I must be mad to let you see what you've done to me and so put another weapon in your hands.

"But what does it matter now? You've done your worst. I only wish I knew just how much damage you've done, but I doubt if I ever will."

"I've stolen nothing," she cried. "I have never told anybody here anything about your carriage. If I had, I could have told them that our steering needs to be improved, because yours is smoother. But I've told them nothing. I swear it. Please, you must believe me."

"Believe *you?* Are you mad? Now, listen to me, for these are the last words we will ever exchange. I said you have done your worst, now I'm going to do mine. I'm going to win that race and win the Prince as a customer.

"Kennington Engineering will lead the world with the horseless carriage, and eventually people will forget that Radford's ever made one. I advise you to stick to railway engines. It's about Radford's level.

"There, now I've said all I have to say to you, and everything is over between us. After today I hope I never have to see or speak to you again."

With that, he walked out of the room, leaving her devastated.

She sank into a chair, while harsh sobs wracked her. She knew that he would never have spoken such cruel, cutting words to her if she had not hurt him beyond bearing, but they were still terrible.

After a while she raised her head and forced her tears to stop. Today she must think only of her duty. She could cry later. She could cry all night and all the following day. But she must not cry now.

When she walked back to the other room she was quite composed. Only a faint pallor in her face betrayed her. A quick glance at the Earl showed that he too was pale. He did not look up at her.

It was like that through the lunch that followed. Dorina found herself sitting next to the Prince of Wales. At any other time this would have thrilled her, but now she found his jocular references to her 'little affair' with the Earl very hard to bear.

"You must be sure to invite me to the wedding," he said.

Dorina drew a sharp breath.

"There will be so wedding, sir."

"Really? Do I detect undercurrents?"

"Shoals and rapids," she said. "All of them dangerous."

"Ah! Well, I suspected something of the kind."

At last the meal was over and the company rose to leave the house.

At the starting point of the race they found the mechanics waiting with the vehicles, guarding them jealously.

They had been served lunch in a separate room, which Dorina thought very unfair since it was their hard work that had made all this possible. But Lord Glandon, whose social attitudes were very lofty, would not have dreamed of sitting down at the same table as mechanics.

Suddenly Dorina became aware that her workers were looking worried.

"Where's Jeremiah?" Mr. Johnson said worriedly. "He returned to the house ten minutes ago, heading for the kitchen. He wanted another slice of the excellent apple cake we had at lunch. But he should have returned by now. He's got to get in and drive."

At that moment a lad in the uniform of a page boy came running from the house.

"It's Mr. Conway," he said breathlessly. "He was

leaving the kitchen and he took the wrong door and fell down the cellar steps."

Everyone exclaimed in concern.

"Is it a long drop?" Dorina asked. "Has poor Mr. Conway been badly hurt?"

"No, ma'am. He talking to us, but he thinks he's broken his leg. He says it hurts badly."

"Send for the doctor immediately," Lord Glandon said.

Dorina's eyes met Mr. Johnson's in horror.

"You'd better go and see him, my dear," the kindly Prince told her.

It took only a moment for her to descend the cellar steps and ascertain that the page boy had been right. Jeremiah Conway had sustained no head injuries, but his leg was badly hurt.

"I'm so sorry to let you down," he moaned. "I don't know who's going to drive now."

"Never mind that," Dorina told him. "The doctor is on his way and you must think about nothing but getting well."

Having ensured that someone was staying with him, she hurried back to the starting point of the race.

The Prince expressed his concern for Mr. Conway, before saying,

"Does this mean that our race cannot take place?"

"No, sir," Dorina said at once. "I shall drive the vehicle myself."

There was a buzz. Nobody had considered such a thing possible.

"Miss Radford," Mr. Johnson said in consternation, "you cannot simply get in and drive without any instruction."

"Of course not," she told him. "But I'm a very good driver."

"But how – ?"

"It would take too long to go into now. Believe me when I say that I can drive."

Looking up, she saw the Prince regarding her quizzically and she had the feeling that he understood a good deal.

"Well then," he said. "That's settled."

"It's impossible!"

Everybody turned and looked at the Earl, who had spoken.

"I can take no part in this," he said.

"But why not, my dear fellow?" the Prince enquired.

The Earl took a deep breath.

"I will not race against a lady," he said. "I'm sure that Your Royal Highness would not ask me to."

"But surely that depends on the lady," the Prince said. "She says she can drive. Do you have some reason to think that she is not telling the truth?"

When the Earl seemed unable to answer, Dorina said,

"Lord Kennington knows better than anyone that I *am* telling the truth. In fact, I've been taught by a master."

"Then that's settled," the Prince said, beaming.

"Sir, I cannot race against a lady."

"Any lady or just this lady?" Dorina asked, confronting him.

In a low voice he said,

"Stop this at once, do you hear?"

"I will not stop it," she said in the same voice. "Are you crying off, my Lord?"

"Don't talk nonsense."

"You said you were going to do your worst. Now I shall do mine. I'm going to win this race and then we'll see who should stick to railway engines."

"I will not race you."

"The race is mine then, and all that goes with it."

He went pale.

"I think not," he said, "since it is you that has lost your driver."

"And have replaced him with another. I'm ready to start. It is *you* who are backing out."

In desperation the Earl turned to Mr. Johnson.

"Surely you have someone else who can drive?" he demanded.

"It's not his decision, it's mine," Dorina said firmly before Mr. Johnson could reply.

But he touched her arm nervously.

"Wouldn't it be better if – ?

"No," she told him. *"I* make the decisions here."

He backed off, startled by how like her father she had looked at that moment.

"Stand back," Dorina said to the little crowd around her vehicle.

As they moved away she climbed into the driving seat.

"I'm ready, my Lord," she called to the Earl, "unless, of course, you're afraid of the competition."

That did it. His lips tightened and he leapt into the driving seat of his own carriage.

"Ready?" cried Lord Glandon. "Then the race has begun."

Two men cranked up the engines until they hummed, then hastily got out of the way. The next instant both carriages glided forward.

For the first few moments Dorina was nervous, but then she began to feel how sweetly the vehicle moved, and knew that she could handle it.

She went a little faster, then faster still. It felt wonderful.

Out of the corner of her eye she could see that the Earl was keeping neck and neck with her. A slight bend in the road was coming up and he suddenly accelerated so that he reached it first and was round it while she was still approaching.

That was useful, she thought, since she would not have liked to race him round a bend. On the other hand, he was now well ahead.

The spectators were travelling across country by carriage, so that they could get ahead of the race and watch them approach. Dorina could see the Prince's carriage, with the Prince himself surveying the race.

She speeded up and to her delight caught up with the Earl fairly easily. She managed to get round the next bend ahead of him.

But another bend approached almost at once. Turning the steering wheel she discovered that it had stiffened. It did not seem to respond well and suddenly she realised that she could not turn properly into the bend.

She wrenched frantically at the wheel, but nothing happened. The next moment she had hit the grass verge, careered forward and struck a large stone. The force of the impact overturned the carriage and threw her out.

The Earl, following just behind, saw everything and gasped with horror. He forgot that this woman was his enemy and forgot that he had vowed revenge on her. Nothing mattered as long as she was all right.

He brought his own carriage to a halt so sharply that he too was almost thrown. The next moment he had leapt to the ground and was running to the figure that lay, frighteningly still, on the ground.

"Dorina! *Dorina!*"

He threw himself down beside her, afraid to touch her, yet terrified that she did not move. Her eyes were closed and her face was dreadfully pale.

"Dorina," he whispered, reaching out to lay his finger tips against her face. "Oh dear God! Please wake up, my darling. *Please.*"

The agony in his voice reached her and she turned her head, opening her eyes. Seeing his face leaning over her, she forgot everything except how much she loved him.

"Hello," she said weakly smiling.

"Thank heavens!" he said fervently.

"What happened?" she asked, struggling to get up. "Ouch!"

She had managed to prop herself up on her elbow, but she ached all over, and would have fallen back, except that his arms went around her and he cradled her against him.

"You could have been killed," he said hoarsely.

"It was the steering," she whispered. "I did say yours was better."

"To blazes with the steering!" he said violently.

"But you've won."

"What does that matter? What does anything matter, as long as you're all right?"

"I'm sorry I deceived you, but I didn't spy on you. Truly I didn't. It was just a muddle and it all got out of my control. You do believe me don't you?"

"Yes, yes," he said frantically. "As long as you're not seriously hurt I don't care about anything else. *Oh, my darling!"*

With these words he pulled her tighter and buried his face against her. Moving carefully, Dorina managed to get one arm about him, to touch his head with caressing fingers.

"I love you," she said.

"And I love you, always and forever. My darling, what would I have done if you'd been killed? Forgive me for everything I said."

"It was my fault," she assured him, "all my fault. I should never have deceived you in the first place – "

"Such an innocent deception," he broke in quickly. "I should have been more understanding. But I'll make it up to you. I'll spend my whole life making it up to you, if only you'll forgive me."

"There is nothing to forgive," she murmured. "Let us put it behind us and think only of the future."

Behind them they heard the sounds of the others approaching, exclaiming consternation.

"Don't move," the Earl told her, "in case you have any broken bones."

"No, I don't think so. Just bruises. I can stand up."

Clinging to him, she managed to rise. But as soon as she was on her feet, he lifted her in his arms.

"Over here, old fellow," the Prince called, indicating his own carriage. "We'll soon have her back to the house to see the doctor."

Tenderly the Earl helped Dorina into the carriage and got in beside her. The Prince regarded them benignly.

"No serious damage?" he asked.

"Nothing very much, thank you, sir," she said.

"Except that you lost the race. I'm afraid I shall be taking Kennington's carriage now."

"I'm glad," she said at once. "Besides, after this, Radford's and Kennington's will be teaming up, so it's all the same thing."

"Ah! Like that is it? In that case – stop the carriage."

Before everyone's incredulous eyes, the Prince of Wales opened the door and climbed out, leaving Dorina and the Earl alone.

"It's a lovely day, Glandon," he boomed. "I think I'll take a gentle stroll back to the house."

He paused just long enough to give Dorina a wink, and then wandered off in the other direction.

As the carriage began to move the Earl enclosed Dorina in his arms again.

"My darling," he said, "I might so easily have lost you."

"Oh no," she said. "You will never lose me. Never in all my life."

"Nor in mine," he said fervently. "I've found you at last, I'm going to make you mine, and nothing will ever come between us again."

Then he drew her gently to him for the kiss she had dreamed of and which heralded the start of their new life together.